The Journal

Of

Daniel Peaster

By

Genea Barmore

Order this book online at www.trafford.com
or email orders@trafford.com

Most Trafford titles are also available at major online book retailers.

Note for Librarians: A cataloguing record for this book is available from Library
and Archives Canada at www.collectionscanada.ca/amicus/index-e.html

Printed in Victoria, BC, Canada.

ISBN: 978-1-4251-9180-1(sc)
ISBN: 978-1-4251-9182-5 (e-book)

*Our mission is to efficiently provide the world's finest, most comprehensive
book publishing service, enabling every author to experience success.
To find out how to publish your book, your way, and have it available
worldwide, visit us online at www.trafford.com*

Trafford rev. 10/05/2009

 www.trafford.com

North America & international
toll-free: 1 888 232 4444 (USA & Canada)
phone: 250 383 6864 ♦ fax: 812 355 4082

Chapter 1

City of Carthage, June 8, 1920

Caleb Bizzle, parked his car in front of the Hanson building, where his detective agency is located on the third floor. He didn't see the car's of his partner's, Lyle Bertram and Earl Caine, around. He had worked with them at the McNair agency years before they decided to begin their own agency. They were retired police and they liked his idea of keeping their own fees, minus the office overhead, instead of the percentage they were making at McNair's. Between the three, their finances improved. It was a great help to Lyle as he still had a family to provide for.

Bizzle liked them and they worked together on several assignments. They kept the place going when he went to war. He barely served five months when he was hit by shrapnel. His leg was so mangled he feared they would have to amputate. His situation improved with therapy, he walked out of the hospital with a slight limp six months later. He went back to work with no problem, even with the war, husbands and wives still cheated on each other and wanted proof for their divorce settlements. It was as if he'd never left.

He was returning from an assignment involving him spying on a cheating husband. He had handed over all the proof of his labors to the wife, who was amorously appreciative. She also gave him an extra one hundred dollars for his trouble. He waved to a passerby as he unloaded his grip from the backseat. He stopped at the news stand and bought a box of cigars. Ole Charlie commented on his cheerful disposition. Caleb only smiled and gave him a dollar tip. He headed up stairs and walked into a phone conversation his secretary Billie was engaging. She smiled at him as he passed. "No, Mr. Wilson, he hasn't come in yet. I've told you before I 'm not exactly sure when he'll arrive. Yes, sir, I'll tell him as soon as I see him. Goodbye."

Billie replaced the receiver and walked into Bizzle's office. "So, you made it back." Caleb smiled. "I missed you, as well, doll." He was unpacking his camera and extra shirts. Billie helped gather up his laundry to send to the cleaners. She held up a photo of a couple engaged in a torrid kiss. "My!" she gasped. Bizzle grabbed the picture from her, "You're to young to be looking at things like that."

She made a face at him. "Did she pay you or do I need to send a statement?" Bizzle grinned. Billie rolled her eyes. "As a matter of fact, she paid." Billie smiled at him, "She must've been very pleased with your work." Bizzle began humming and sat down at his desk leaning back in his chair lighting one of his cigars. "Oh, my Billie girl, I'm tired. I thought of taking a little vacation." Billie gave out a snort. "Lotta good that'll do. Every time you say that some big case lands in your lap and you're off and running."

She sat down on the corner of his desk looking at him. He did look tired but that didn't take anything away from his handsome features. It only made her love him more. "Why the face, Billie?" She startled at his voice, she looked into his deep blue tormented eyes. "Nothing, only wool gathering." She stood up and smoothed her dress. "I'm going to take these to the laundry and bring back lunch." "Where are the others?"He asked. "Out on assignment." Bizzle nodded.

Poor Billie, he thought to himself. Always there for him and why he couldn't figure. He wished she would go find herself a beau and get married. She was a good looking girl but she didn't have emerald green eyes and auburn hair. Caleb stretched and rubbed his tired eyes he looked out the window and saw the clouds moving in on a bright day. A fierce clap of thunder rattled the panes. There was a knock at the door. Bizzle turned to see a small astute man waiting.

"Hello. May I come in." Bizzle lay his cigar in the ashtray and stood up. "Yes. May I help you?" The little man smiled, "I guess your secretary forgot about me." Bizzle didn't remember seeing anyone in the lobby. "I apologize, please." He motioned at the chair in front of his desk. "I won't take much of your time. I am William Calloway, attorney at law. I represent Emily Will." Bizzle's eyes widened. "Emily!" William Calloway rested his briefcase on his lap and retrieved a legal looking paper. Bizzle sat on the corner of his desk and took the document the attorney offered. "She has instructed me to inform you that she has named you executor of her estate.

Bizzle closed his eyes tight. "She's dead." "On the contrary, Mr. Bizzle. She would also like to see you. She wants your help." Bizzle looked at him puzzled. "What for?" "I'm not at liberty to say. She wants to tell you in person. Due to her present condition she is unable to travel. She would like for you to visit as soon as possible. Bizzle thought out loud. "Why would she name me executor." William Calloway snapped shut his briefcase and stood.

"Shall I tell her you will see her?" He peered at Bizzle. "Of course." Calloway handed his another piece of paper. "Here is the address and directions to the house. If you leave directly you can be there by tomorrow morning." Bizzle nodded his head at what Mr. Calloway was saying only his mind was reeling of hearing Emily's name again and that she wanted to see him. Mr. Calloway interrupted him, "Mr. Bizzle. I'll let her know you are on your way?"

Bizzle snapped back from his thoughts, "Of course, Mr. Calloway." They shook hands, Mr. Calloway was at the door when he turned to Bizzle. "It is most urgent, Mr. Bizzle." Bizzle nodded, "Yes, sir." He was alone now and opened one of the bottles of scotch a previous client supplied him with and poured out a drink. *"Get a hold of yourself, Bizzle. How long has it been? Six years."* He swallowed the scotch in one gulp.

Two hours later, Billie returned with lunch. She put her things down and saw that Caleb's door was open. She walked over to his desk to find the note he left.

Billie,

Something important came up. I don't know when I'll return.

Caleb

She, sank into his chair, angry. "Dammit!"

CHAPTER 2

As Bizzle drove his thoughts wandered to Emily and the first time he saw her. He was to meet a client at the Halifax hotel. Lounging at the counter, he waited, while the desk clerk checked to see if his client had checked in. A giggle caught his attention and he turned. He couldn't breathe when he saw her. Sitting there in the lobby on a sofa was the woman of his dreams. She had auburn hair surrounding creamy white skin, when she happened to look up in his direction there were emerald green eyes peering out under her hat.

The desk clerk had to tap his arm to get his attention. "He left a message, sir." Bizzle scanned the note saying his client would have to postpone. His eyes wandered back to the woman. He couldn't take his eyes off of her. At last he beckoned the desk clerk and asked if he knew who she was. He was disappointed to hear Mrs. Will then he brightened, she could be a widow. He had to speak to her. Luckily her friend, who he would come to know as Patty, stood up and walked towards the back of the lobby where dry goods were sold.

He strolled over and watched as the woman cast an eye in his direction. He thought she would be annoyed or act indifferent as most women but she looked right at him and gave him a most charming smile. He tipped his hat and asked if the seat by her was taken. She began to protest but he sat down before she could say anything.

"My name is Caleb Bizzle. How do you do? She smiled apprehensively, "Fine. And yourself?"

"Very well, thank you. Are you visiting here?"

"Yes, as a matter of fact."

"How do you like it, so far?"

"I only arrived last night. My friend, Patty, and I are going sight seeing today."

"I imagine you'll need a guide?'

"Not exactly, she's a local." She smiled at his disappointed, "Oh." Bizzle thought, "So, I suppose you'll be out all day?'

"At least until six, she has to work tonight."

Bizzle brightened, "That's a shame, what will you do for dinner?"

"Eat, I suppose." Clever, he acknowledged.

"That's good. I eat here occasionally myself, perhaps I'll join you."

"Perhaps." she smiled at him. "Good, I'll see you tonight." He walked away as if he were leaving then dashed around the corner and waited. Her friend, Patty, had returned and she was telling her what had occurred. "You don't think he sent someone to watch me." Emily sounded frightened. "Don't be silly, maybe it made him feel good to talk to a pretty girl." Emily nervously giggled. "He didn't want to know my name."

"Honey, they rarely do. C'mon lets go." He watched them leave and thought to himself. *"I want to know everything, about you."*

Chapter 3

Bizzle pulled into a station and told the attendant to fill 'er up. He went inside and grabbed a couple books of matches. He thought about putting a call into Billie but changed his mind. He stood by while the attendant washed his windshield. "Heard it was gonna storm in a couple of hours." He told Bizzle there was a nice motel in the next town if he wanted to dodge the rain. He paid the man and thanked him.

He was just outside of the city limits when the storm hit. He could barely see in front of him, he slowed to a snails pace. Another mile and he saw the lights for the motel. After checking in and buying a sandwich and coffee he sloshed his way to his room.

Stripping off his soaked clothes and hanging them up he put on his bathrobe and sat down to eat. He tried to find a station on the little radio but he only picked up static, every once in a while the lights flickered as the thunder rolled overhead.

Bizzle unwrapped one of the glasses provided and dug from his suitcase the pint of scotch. Stretching out on the squeaky bed he sipped at it and remembered his dinner with Emily. She was seated in the hotel restaurant ordering. Bizzle hurried over. "Good evening." Her eyes widened. He motioned at the chair beside her, "May I." She only nodded. He told the waiter what he wanted and picked up his water glass tipping his head in her direction.

"I didn't think you were serious."

"How's that."

"I didn't think you would show."

"And miss an opportunity to dine with the most sublime female I've ever seen."

"You are awfully bold. I don't think this is a good idea." She tried to stand but he put his hand on hers. "Don't go, Mrs. Will, please." She sat back down. "How do you know my name? He has you following me, doesn't he."

"Who?"

"You know very well."

"I'm sorry, I don't. My wanting to know you is all my own idea." He smiled at her and saw how tense she was. "I know your name because I asked the desk clerk. Nobody sent me, please, believe me."

She thought for a moment and began to relax. "Alright, Mr. Bizzle, if that is how you want to do this. He smiled at her, "Call me Caleb. She nodded. "Might I ask your name?"

She laughed, "I thought you already knew." He shook his head, "The clerk only gave your last name. The missus part, are you married or a widow?" She paused for a moment. "Let's just say it is a marriage of convenience."

"I see."

"No, you don't but let's let it be for now."

"Very well." Their order arrived and Bizzle dove in, Emily ate timidly watching him.

Between bites he managed to ask her, "Did you enjoy your day?"

"Yes, the city is bigger than I remember."

"So, you lived here before?"

"A long time ago."

"I've lived here all my life.

"What line of work are you in?" Bizzle grinned with a mouth full of food. "Well, don't panic, but I am a private detective." Her eyes widened. "Don't panic, I'm being honest with you." She looked at him suspiciously then her frown began to ease. He figured, she was either, believing him or trying to trap him in a lie.

"What sort of a detective are you, I mean, what have been some of your cases."

He wiped his mouth with his napkin and thought, "Oh, tracking down relatives who had an inheritance coming to them. Catching the cheating husband or wife in the act. I even found a little girl who was thought to have been kidnaped but she had only wandered off, that family was very grateful."

"So, you travel quite a bit, I imagine."

"Sometimes, usually just here and some of the surrounding cities." He finished his meal and emptied his coffee cup. "Would you like to see a play or go hear some music?" She fussed with her napkin, "I don't think I should, I wouldn't want your report to say anymore than it does."

"Report!" He was surprised. "What can I say or do to convince you no one hired me" He implored. She gazed into his hurt eyes and he saw the tears well in hers. "Good night, Mr. Bizzle." She hurried out of the restaurant before he could stop her. *'Poor kid'* he thought as he laid out the money for dinner. He walked around to the flower shop on the corner and had a bouquet sent to her room. On the note he wrote:

No one hired me, I would follow you anywhere for nothing.

See you, tomorrow, Caleb.

He reached the restaurant in the morning to find her sitting alone sipping a cup of coffee. She was startled by his voice and turned to him. "Good morning." He bowed to her. "May I sit with you?" He saw how tired she looked but she relented and said yes. "Did you receive my flowers?" She nodded, "Very nice. Have some coffee." He poured a cup.

"Will your friend, Patty, be joining us?"

"Actually, I'll join her later when she calls. She works nights and needs her sleep."

"You're up early, you're supposed to relax on vacation."

"When you have two boys you have to get up early to get them on their way, I'm used to it."

"Oh, you have two sons."

"You seem disappointed."

"Not at all. How old are they."

"Ten, they're twins."

"Identical?"

"Fraternal."

"You don't look old enough to have either."

"I was very young.

"I imagine they're a handful."

"At times."

"I suppose your husband is having a time of it while you're away."

"He doesn't have much to do with them, besides our house keeper is looking after them."

"Housekeeper! Your husband must be well off." She only nodded.

"Would you like some breakfast?"

"Why are you doing this?'

"Doing what?"

"This. You know I have a husband and children and that doesn't deter you in the least."

"I can't explain it. I saw you and fell in love. I'd like to spend as much time with you, as I, possibly can."

"In love. You're in love with me?" She shook her head rubbing her forehead wearily.

"Is that so hard to believe?" She didn't answer. "I don't expect anything from you. Years from now I'll be able to look back fondly on how I spent a glorious time with a mysterious lovely young woman." He leaned toward her to see what she was thinking. She looked at him with moist eyes still unsure.

"I'm not so mysterious or lovely." He took her hand. "Believe me, you are. I know." He said the last with such conviction she giggled. She looked at him for a long moment he melted in her gaze. "Emily." He was caught off guard, "Pardon." She smiled, "My name is Emily." He leaned back proud of himself and smiled. "Emily."

He seemed at a loss for words looking about the table. "By the way, what made you change your mind."

"You were truthful about being a detective."

"How do you know?'

"Looked you up in the phone book. How much did you pay, for an ad of that size?"

"Enough, believe me. Would you like breakfast now?'

She nodded, "You have quite an appetite."

"I've been working hard these two days, what do you expect?" She laughed as he hailed the waiter.

CHAPTER 4

CALEB GROANED AS HE rolled over stretching out his arms he accidentally knocked the glass from the side table. Hearing it shatter he groaned again, *"Great."* He rolled over peering from the edge of the bed at the shards . He belched and got out on the other side. He picked up his bottle but it was empty. Stumbling into the bathroom he flicked on the light, everything looked yellow. *'What are you doing to yourself, Bizzle?'* He disgustedly looked at his reflection in the mirror. He climbed into the tub and took a long hot shower.

After buying a cup of coffee and two donuts, his suitcase packed and in the car, he settled in and drove. It was a bright beautiful morning. Rolling down the windows to let the fresh air hit him, it was sweet after the storm, his mood began improving. He saw a road sign that read Pierce sixty miles. He noticed that the radiator was over heating. He found a gas station and pulled in. He went to the little café and ordered a sandwich while the attendant serviced his car. He stood by while the boy was checking his tires.

"Goin' far, mister?" The boy was wiping his hands on his pants with a friendly grin on his face. "Pierce." Bizzle said and the boys eyes widened. "You have relations there, mister?"

"No. Why?"

"Just askin', heard on the news some big fire broke out at old man Will's." Bizzle stood up straight. "Anybody hurt?"

"Don't know. Last I know they're still trying to put it out."

"Who's old man Will?"

"Oh he's a mean old guy, built the town, has a big house." He grinned, "Had a big house, I mean."

"Mean, huh?"

"Yeah, people say he's killed but nobody could do anything."

"Couldn't? Or wouldn't?"

"Not much difference. He owned the whole town and everybody in it."

"Everybody?" Bizzle teased.

"Purt near, the ones that crossed him weren't never heard from again."

"I'll be. Did he have family?"

"Yeah, but they're just as mean. Says his wife won't show her face in town. Doesn't want to mingle with the pissants." Bizzle smiled, "Don't you mean peasants?" The boy thought, then grinned and shrugged his shoulders. Bizzle asked how much further while he was paying the boy told him another thirty miles. He thanked him and drove on.

Bizzle tried to make sense out of his chat with the attendant. So, Emily's husband owned the whole town, and he was mean. Why would Emily act that way she was a very kindly person when he knew her. He stopped himself, '*there you go again trying to create something out of a smattering of gossip.*' Bizzle straightened up in his seat and cleared his throat. '*Just wait till you get there.*'

Dark clouds were rolling in, when Bizzle reached the city limits of Pierce, it began to sprinkle. He could see black smoke above the town. He slowed the car to see the activities. In spite of the rain there were people lining the sidewalks, it looked like they were celebrating. He almost hit the car in front of him that had come to a complete stop. He leaned out the window trying to see what had stopped them.

People of all sizes and ages milling back and forth, some had mugs of beer they were toasting to other people they passed. He overheard some of what was being said. "Couldn't happen to a nicer bunch, if you ask me." "Serves them right, the way they treated us." He over heard an older woman raring her head, "After all the misery that bastard has caused." Another citizen stated, "And those two boys, made my skin crawl just to see them."

On and on it went as they passed. Bizzle realized the cars in front of him weren't going to move anytime soon so he pulled around them. He slowly made his way down the main street stopping often for folks with no particular destination in mind. After about four blocks the crowds had all migrated down the street he could hear the music of the band he saw setting up on the sidewalk beginning to play. He could still see the smoke and picking up speed he followed it until he was parked in front of the iron fence of the estate. The fire trucks were set around the house in strategic locations as the men fought the blaze. The house was enormous from what he could tell. The rain was coming down harder. It looked to Bizzle as though it was helping to extinguish the blaze.

Every once in awhile a carload of people would drive by cheering. It bothered him, yet his curiosity about old man Will and his family causing such feelings in the town out weighed his annoyance. He saw a serious looking police officer waving the cars on past the house. As the storm continued the traffic dissipated. That was when he noticed Bizzle standing by his car. He called over another officer, spoke with him briefly and then headed over towards Bizzle. "I'm Chief Elliot Banes, are you a reporter?" Bizzle handed him his card, "No sir, My name is Caleb Bizzle, I'm a private investigator from Carthage..." Banes interrupted him, we have every thing under control, we don't need an investigator ... " Bizzle raised his hand. "You don't understand Chief, an attorney, William Calloway contacted me yesterday that Emily Will wanted to talk to me." "About what?" Chief Banes asked. "He wasn't at liberty to say".

Banes wiped his nose. "How do you know her?" "I met her a few years back."

"Kept in contact with her." Bizzle looked at his feet. "Not exactly." Banes nodded, "I see. So she calls out of the blue, you drop everything, and here you are." Bizzle was becoming irritated. "Is that so unusual?" Banes retreated. "Not at all. Just getting the pieces together." Banes leaned in for a closer look at Bizzle's coat lapel. "I see your pin , you over there?" Bizzle looked at his lapel. "Yes, sir. Took some shrapnel, medical discharge with honor's" Banes almost smiled. " It doesn't look like there is much more I can do here until the fire chief declares the fire is completely out. Lets go over to the café I need a cup of coffee." Bizzle nodded that would be fine by him. He smiled as he heard Banes mutter on his way to the car that the rain wasn't helping his cold any.

Once they were settled at a table, Banes told the waiter to bring two cups of coffee. He excused himself and headed toward the back of the café, Bizzle saw him use the telephone. He gazed out the window at the pouring rain. Most of the crowds had disappeared, he could hear the band in the distance, '*Probably found a bar.*' He thought. Banes returned as the waiter was serving their coffee. "Any word if they found anybody?" Banes looked at him, "Oh, the phone call. No. I called Calloway." "Oh?" Banes waved him off, "Procedure."

He wiped his nose again and sipped his coffee. "Whose car was that parked by that little house?"Bizzle asked. "That belonged to Mr. Will."

"Belonged? Is he dead?"

"Doubt it. He was arrested in Carthage, yesterday." Bizzle sat back stunned.

"Haven't seen the paper?"

"No. No I haven't."

"So, you're a detective." Bizzle nodded. "How did you get into that line of work?"

"My father was a detective. He died when I was seventeen. I took his place at McNair's."

"Why did you quit?"

"The original owner was a fair man when he retired his nephew took over. He was young and college educated only he was more interested in the money than the investigation. Wouldn't reimburse us if we happened to go over budget. Of course, the budget was so small, it couldn't be helped. So two others, that had, had enough, and myself, began our own agency."

"Business good?"

"It's growing. We're better off than we were."

"I can see that."Banes agreed. "You always been a police officer?" Bizzle asked.

"Huh? No. I went to college with the hopes of going to work for the department of justice. As usual, life changes your perspective. My dad died almost a week after graduation. He was never a well man. So I was responsible for my mother. I hired on with the police force in Bantree where I grew up. I made lieutenant, then the war. When I returned the old police chief Cole here died and everyone thought I'd be perfect for the job."

"So much for the department of justice."Bizzle said. Banes shrugged. "After the war I thought it best to stay here. I moved my mother here and settled into small town life."

"Are you happy here?"

"As happy as I'll ever be, I imagine." Bizzle left it at that and changed the subject.

"So you grew up around here. What do you know about Mr. Will?"

"I mainly heard stories when we would visit relatives or they would visit us. I'd heard that if someone crossed Mr. Will, sooner or later something of theirs would mysteriously catch fire."

"What did Cole do?"

"Not a lot. Everyone knew, who set the fires, only there was never any evidence and never any witnesses."

"Just a lot of coincidence."

"Too much coincidence if you ask me."

"Anything happen since you've been here?"

"No. It's been fairly calm until today."

"You ever meet Mr. Will?"

" I never laid eyes on him until I took over here and he came to see me. He wasn't pleased that the town council hired me without his input. He's, an intimidating man, to say the least."

"Sizing you up, I suspect."

" He asked about my qualifications and so on then he shook my hand and said something that struck me odd.. He said that since the good people of this community saw fit to hire me, to do a good job. " If it's one thing I cannot abide, it is paying someone to do a job, such as being the chief of police, and come to find that they are doing that job poorly." Considering, everyone thought Cole was in his pocket I wondered why he would give me such advice."

Bizzle pondered what Banes had told him. "Did you investigate Mr. Will?"

"No reason to. It wasn't until the newspaper came out that lent any insight into Mr. Will's world. It wouldn't have done any good to have inquired about him since he used alias' where ever he went."

"Who turned him in?"

"His own employee, Daniel Peaster. He was the school teacher at Will's place. Anyhow, after Peaster gave exclusive interviews to all the newspapers in Carthage it was revealed that Thomas Will was actually Thomas Arbaugh."

"What charges did they have on him?"

"Arson and murder. He burnt down his parents home when he was ten, they died in the fire. He was sent to the insane asylum. He was there for a year when he escaped. They searched for him to no avail."

"So no one knew what he looked like once he was grown."

"Nope. Changed his name and none were the wiser."

"Now, this Daniel Peaster. What's his story?"

"You know that little house the car was parked by?" Bizzle nodded. "That was Mr. Peaster's cottage. Next to it was a school house. I understood, Mr. Will hired him to teach the twins because they were so far from the school here in town. There were a few other children that lived in the vicinity that attended."

"What was Peaster like?"

"I met him once and saw him in town occasionally. He was polite enough, but there was something I didn't like."

"Such as?"

"Can't really say. Just something about him. Then he goes and turns Mr. Will in to the authorities. I don't know what happened between them to cause it."

"What did Mr. Will do for a living?"

"Shipping mostly. He owns quite a few of the barges plus I believe he owns a few freighters."

"I wonder where he got his money to begin with?" Banes shrugged. "Couldn't say."

Banes leaned forward. "Didn't Emily tell you any of this?" Bizzle cleared his throat. "No. She didn't speak about her personal life. I knew she was afraid of him."

"She say why?" Bizzle shook his head. Banes lowered his voice. "Just what was your relationship with her?" Bizzle thought for a moment. "For me, Chief, it was love at first sight. She was sure I'd been hired to follow her while she was visiting in Carthage. I was persistent in convincing her I wasn't and we spent two wonderful weeks together."

"So, why did her attorney have to track you down?"

"We had made plans to marry. She wanted to come back and get her sons. She made me swear that I wouldn't do anything until I heard from her. A couple of times I wrote to her addressing them with phoney names to avoid suspicion, she never answered me. She never sent for me."

"Weren't you curious what happened."

"At first. Then I began feeling sorry for myself, that she was only having a fling and playing a game. Then the war began and

I went, mainly thinking I'd forget."

"Didn't work, did it?"

"Sure as hell didn't"

"She must have some feelings for you or she wouldn't have named you her executor.

"True."

An officer strode up to the table to report that the fire chief declared the area contained. Banes nodded to Bizzle. "This is where my work begins." "May I come with you?" Banes grabbed his hat. "Sure."

Reaching the scene Banes is met by the fire chief Ted Whitlock. Ted gave Bizzle a once over and looked at Banes. "He's okay." Bizzle offered his hand. "Good to meet you." Ted reciprocated. "You too." With the introductions over Ted began. "We've found a couple of bodies." Bizzle's heart sank. He followed Banes and Ted under the tent. Ted pulled back the tarp. Two scorched corpses lay before them. "What do you think?" Banes asked. "I, think it's, the twins." Ted said.

"How's that?"

"Their clothes or what's left of them are identical. If you look at their left hands, you'll see the rings." Banes knelt down to examine them. Both were wearing pinkie rings with an engraved 'W' on them. "Where did you find them?" Ted indicated that they were found in the vicinity of the front room. "This one was by the sofa. This one was a few feet away lying opposite of the other."

"Did you have to get them out from under a beam?"

"No. Just rubble."

"I think you're right the clothing matches one another."

"They were fraternal, weren't they?" Bizzle asked. Ted answered. "Yeah, why?"

"Isn't it strange, they're grown and they still dress alike?" Ted thought. "Humph. Couldn't say. Only when I saw them they were always dressed alike. Besides that the only thing identical about them was they were both ugly and weird." A couple of officers snickered.

"Alright!" Banes interrupted. "Get these two to the morgue for Dr. Jacobs to have a look at." The officers began loading the bodies. Ted was scratching his head. "Don't we know how they died?" Banes shook his head. "I'm not so sure." Ted shrugged. Bizzle approached Banes. "Did you see their skulls." Bizzle nodded. "I think we have ourselves a murder." They were interrupted when Ted called. "We found another one!" They waited while the next body was laid on the tarp.

"This one isn't burned as badly." Banes knelt beside the body. "This is Daniel Peaster. Where did you find him?" Ted pointed to the back of the house. "Outside on the back porch." Banes was counting the slash marks on Peaster's sleeve that led up to both his hands grasping the knife handle sticking out of his chest.

"Good night.' Ted exclaimed. 'What the hell happened around here." Banes stood up and ordered the officers to rope off the area. "This is now a murder scene."

"So chief, the twins killed Peaster?" Ted asked. "I don't know. Could be?" Ted left the group for a moment. Banes looked at Bizzle. "Then who killed the twins?"

Police Chief Elliot Banes and private investigator Caleb Bizzle stood quietly deep in thought. Banes startled Bizzle. "I'd like your help."Banes said. "Of course, Chief."

"In light of this, let's go down to the cottage and have a look around." Banes informed one of the officers where he would be and they started for the cottage. Approaching the small house they stopped and observed the place. "Look at those marks on the door." Bizzle pointed out. Banes ran his fingers along the grooves. "I wonder what made these." He looked past the door. The marks were on the walls as well. They traced the marks all the way around the cottage back to the door.

Banes turned the knob and slowly opened it. They both stepped inside the dim room. Banes flashed his light slowly from one end of the room to the other. "Nothing seems out of place." Bizzle agreed then stopped Banes as the light hit the door. "Look." He pushed the door closed and shined the light on the now drying blood. Bizzle stood by the door. "Looks like most of the blood came from head wounds." Banes nodded. "As tho someone was knocking someone's head against the door."

"What do you mean, someone. It was Peaster."Bizzle said.

"Could be?" Banes said.

"Chief!"

"I'm serious. It could be Peaster's, could be the twins, could be someone else, we don't have enough to begin forming a conclusion. I want to wait for the autopsies." Bizzle let out a weary breath. Banes continued. "I'll have to go to Carthage and talk with Mr. Will." Bizzle looked around the cottage. "Let's have a look at the school house." From the back side they found a rick of wood. Banes pondered the stump used to split the logs.

Coming around to the front Banes opened the door. Looking about nothing looked out of place. Bizzle walked over to Peaster's desk. He pulled open the drawers. "Anything?" Banes asked. Bizzle was busy working on the bottom drawer. "This drawer has a false bottom. He sat out the contents on the desk and opened his pocket knife, prying the thin board up he saw a book.
He pulled the heavy leather bound book up and placed it on the desk. Banes came around the corner of the desk. Bizzle opened the cover to the first page. " Property of Daniel Peaster. Confidential." Bizzle flipped the page. "It looks like an account of his time here." Banes scanned the page. "Could shed some light on the situation. You'll have to read it.'

"Not a problem." An officer knocked as he stepped inside. "We found another one, Chief." He looked at Bizzle when he said it. "Dammit. How many people were in that house!" Banes barked. They followed the officer back to the house. Bizzle had a bad feeling. He took a deep breath as Ted pulled the tarp back. "Emily!" Bizzle said it louder than he realized.

"Take him outta here." Banes shouted. "No, Chief. Please." He begged, Banes relented. They gathered around her as if to provide a shield. "How do you know it's Emily?" Banes asked. Bizzle swallowed and pointed to her right hand clutching something at her throat. "The broach. I gave her that." Banes looked her over. "I don't see any marks on her like the others." Ted spoke up. "We found her on a lounge chair. She was up on the second floor when it imploded she dropped." Bizzle wiped at his eyes.

Banes knelt down, "What's this on her face?" Ted leaned closer. "Look's like a veil." "Veil?" Bizzle said. Banes grasped a loose corner and began to pull it away but the skin began peeling with it. Everyone jumped as Emily's body heaved. "Oh no. She's alive!" Ted shouted. Men ran for their medical equipment. Bizzle knelt beside her, "Emily! Emily! It's Caleb, I'm here. Emily!" Banes had his finger on her wrist checking for a pulse. One fireman checked her heart beat. They looked at one another. "She's gone." Banes whispered. "No!" Bizzle cried. "I'm sorry." Banes told him then motioned to an officer to lead him away. They began wrapping Emily's body to load in the truck.

Banes waited for Bizzle to collect himself. Bizzle noticed the chief standing there. "You saw it." Banes nodded. "She suffered." Bizzle wept. "I don't think so. It was a muscle spasm. She wasn't alive. I've seen it before." Bizzle looked at him with suspicion. "You're sure." Banes nodded. Bizzle wiped his eyes and nodded. "All right." He paused, "Had you ever seen her,   Chief?"

"No." He said. "She was beautiful, Chief. Why was she wearing a veil?" Banes didn't respond, he thought it best to let Bizzle rant. Bizzle watched as they loaded her into the truck. *"What happened to you, Emily?"* He whispered.

"Maybe it's in that book we found." Banes said. "Yeah." Bizzle took a deep breath. "I need to find a motel." "No. You come with me. My mother will make up the spare room." "I couldn't impose, Chief." "Nonsense. And it's Elliot." Bizzle held out his hand. "Caleb."

Caleb Bizzle was happy to meet Elliot's mother, Silvia. A frail looking woman with a lovely smile. She welcomed him as if he were her own son. She showed him his room and after he was settled he joined them in the kitchen for a meal fit for a king. At first Caleb didn't think he could eat but the aroma awakened his hunger. He felt much better physically afterwards. Elliot folded his napkin and thanked his mother. She smiled at him with a love only a mother could exude.

"I need to get back over there." Elliot lighted a cigarette. "I'll come with you." "No. You need to get started on that book. I need to fill out my report. I'll see you later. Bye, mom."

"Goodbye, son." She smiled at Caleb. "You can read in the living room, if you like. I'll bring you some coffee." "Thank you, Mrs. Banes." Bizzle settled into a comfortable chair, lighted a cigar and opened the book.

CHAPTER 5

The Journal of Daniel Peaster

December 3,1916

It was a miserable day when I arrived in Pierce. *The train ride was dreadful and the rain did little for my attitude, nevertheless, I reached the small town. Looking about while the porter brought out my luggage, I noticed that no one else departed or boarded the train. Soon, the train pulled out and I was left alone. The area of town, I could see, looked, dreary. A few, dim lights, of the shop windows, were visible. Other than that, there was no activity. I reasoned that the rain had something to do with the eeriness of the vicinity, yet, I felt an uneasiness I didn't care for.*

A small, rat faced man, introducing himself as Kranston, explained that he was the manager of the hotel next to the depot and asked if I would like a room. I declined, telling him I was to be met by Mr. Thomas Will. I noticed his beady eyes dim and his thin upper lip curled back, for the briefest moment, at the mention of the name. Composing himself, he offered that I should wait in the lobby where it was warm and have some tea. I thanked him and followed him inside the dank lobby of the Pierce hotel. I took a chair by the fire and my mood improved as I sipped the warm spicy tea and the heat thawed my flesh.

I almost spilt my cup as a scream echoed behind me. I stood to see the manager and a woman embrace. "It's all right, Barbra, just go to the back, he won't be here long." She was visibly trembling as her teary eyes implored his. He squeezed her shoulders reassuringly and she hurried out of sight. Looking about him anxiously, Kranston noticed my concern. "Please, forgive my wife sir, she's a little excited." Quite! I thought, "May I bring you another cup of tea?"

"There is no need for that, Kranston." He spun around so fast at the voice he nearly upset the small table beside him. I looked towards the doorway where the voice sounded and saw the menacing figure. Lightning and thunder, surged overhead adding to the dramatic posture. Apprehensive at the sight I took a breath and asked, "Mr. Thomas Will?" I couldn't make out his features with the dim light and the hood of his cloak drawn down shading his eyes.

The figure stood still for an uncomfortable moment, then he took a step towards me. "Mr. Daniel Peaster, is it?" I extended my hand, he in turn clasped it in a strong icy grip. I stand six feet three and he seemed the same height, yet I felt like a child next to him. He then lowered his hood and I almost gasped. His gaze felt as if it were burning a hole in my body, he looked through you instead of at you and he had a long beard and shoulder length hair, black as midnight. It was the baleful expression that filled me with trepidation.

My usually disciplined composure betrayed me, I shuddered. It was then that he smiled. It did nothing to lessen the severity of his attributes. "You should warm yourself by the fire, Mr. Peaster." His voice suggested mocking. Embarrassed, I changed the subject. "Shall we leave or wait for the storm to ease." He smiled again and looked to Kranston. "I've decided to stay and linger awhile. Not that I mind the storm, you'll get used to our weather, Mr. Peaster, it rains more often that not. Isn't that so, Kranston." The little man jumped, "Oh, yes sir, more often than not."

He nodded at me emphatically. Mr. Will began removing his

cloak and told Kranston to bring him a cup of tea. Kranston turned to leave when he changed his mind. "Instead, have Barbra bring it, I haven't seen her for some time, now." He took the chair opposite mine, "Have a seat, Mr. Peaster." His attention turned to the flames and was silent. I suppose, my fidgeting annoyed him. Still staring at the flames, he asked why I was so nervous. "I am a bit anxious about something in your letter concerning my teaching position." He didn't look away from the fire, "Such as?"

"You explained that your two boys would be my concern as well as any others. I was curious about, the others." He sat up in his chair and focused on me. "Some of my workers have children and it is difficult for them to attend the school here in town, it is so far away. I built the school not only for my boys but for them as well. I expect them to be taught with the same enthusiasm afforded my own. I wasn't fortunate to have any formal education and I won't deny anyone the opportunity, if they so desire."

With that he leaned back and returned his attention to the fire. I commended his decision, by that time, Kranston brought his tea. Mr. Will stood up towering above the nervous man. "I told you, I wanted Barbra to bring it!" Kranston grimaced, "I'm sorry, sir, she is in bed with a terrible headache." Mr. Will smiled, "I should extend my sympathies." Kranston stammered, "That won't be necessary." Mr. Will raised an eyebrow, "I mean to say, you shouldn't bother yourself." He looked almost in tears. "Nonsense, you entertain Mr. Peaster and I'll return, shortly."

With that Mr. Will strode to the back and Kranston collapsed against the wall. I heard a door slam and a faint cry in the distance. Kranston dropped the cup of tea he had brought Mr. Will and slid to the floor covering his ears. He moaned and I went to help him up. "What is going on here, Kranston!" His frightened eyes looked into mine. "Please, forgive me, sir, don't pay any mind." He tried to urge me to my chair. "I don't understand, Kranston." He kept tugging my arm. "It's best you stay out of it, sir." He gave up coercing me and picked up my cup of tea, "Here you are, sir."

He thrust the cup in my hand and stumbled over to the window, trying to change the subject. "It looks as if the rain is letting up." My mind reeled at the events taking place. What had I gotten myself into?" I could see Kranston was speaking to me, "I beg your pardon." He cleared his throat and asked if I was the new school teacher. I told him that I was. Just then the bang of a door slamming open sounded from the back and he looked at me, nervously.

"I hope you last longer than Mr. Collins." I didn't care for the sound of that. Mr. Will charged into the room, a sneer on his lip. "Help Mr. Peaster with his luggage." barking at Kranston who jumped to do his bidding. He gathered his cloak and headed for the door. I, snapped to attention, put on my coat and hat and carried the remaining gear to the carriage. Mr. Will was seated when I climbed in. Barely settled , he slapped the reins and the horses jerked

into motion. Neither of us spoke the entire way. I couldn't since he was driving so fast causing the mud to sling in every direction, especially on me. I tried to pull my hat in such a way to keep the muck away but it was of no use.

I chanced a glimpse in Mr. Will's direction and the sight frightened me. His hood had fallen back, the wind was blowing his wet hair back, his jaw was set and with the mire splattered across his face in such a way he looked like a demon driving. I felt sick as he steered us over narrow slick bridges taking corners so fast, it felt like the carriage would tip over. All the while, he drove the horses, unmercifully.

My one thought was to get out of town, as soon as possible. Of course, I knew it would take time considering I had no money. I tried to console myself that the events of today were of no concern to me. I knew nothing of this town and its history, I was wet, cold and tired and everything was going to look worse than it was. I was judging too soon. I should give it the benefit of the doubt. Once settled, things would look better, especially after a rest.

I didn't think I'd nodded off but a sink hole jolted me out of my drowse. I took out my handkerchief and dabbed at my face. The rain had stopped but it was still overcast. I could see a rooftop looming ahead of us. Drawing nearer, the full scope of Mr. Will's estate came into view. Ivy covered most of the stone facade. It looked to be at

least three floors and as intimidating as Mr. Will. There, were bal-
conies, to all the windows, on the second floor. The grounds were well
maintained and the stables appeared orderly. I was impressed to say
the least.

Just as we were turning onto the drive towards the house, he took
a sharp right turn onto a narrow path. This lead around to two small
structures. He finally halted the horses in front of the second , which
was a small cottage. My legs were so numb I nearly sat in the mud
as I dislodged. I gained my footing and stumbled around to get my
luggage, Mr. Will was already hauling a few things inside. I followed
him in and sat my things down. He was lighting the lamp as I peeled
off my soaking coat and hat.

"Here you are, Mr. Peaster." I looked around at my new dwell-
ing. The furnishings were sparse, (I was never one for clutter), yet I
was very pleased with my surroundings. It was warm and comfortable. "I had Peeler light the fire to take the chill off." He looked at
his pocket watch and checked the clock on the mantle, satisfied they
were synchronized he turned to me. "It's one 'o clock now, I can have
something prepared for you if you're hungry, supper isn't until seven."

I could see a cabinet in the corner with a sink and a stove with
a kettle sitting on top. He followed my gaze. "Oh yes. The previous
occupant, Mr. Collins had that put in, he liked to eat by himself." I
turned to him, then. Undaunted, he walked over to see what was left
in the larder. "Here." He motioned," Biscuits, tea, coffee, help yourself,
Mr. Peaster." "Thank you, I believe I'll wait for supper. A bathe and a
nap will be most welcome, for now." Mr. Will shut the cupboard and
stood before me. The mud was caked on his beard, I'm sure I didn't
look any better.

"Get yourself settled and if you need anything, furnishings, et cetera,
let me know." His demeanor was relaxed compared with earlier, I
didn't know what to make of it. "I thank you, Mr. Will, I will see
you at supper." I smiled cordially as he studied me. 'You're welcome,
Mr. Peaster." He started for the door and stopped. "Mr. Peaster, you
remember what I told you about my boys in the letter?" I thought,
"Yes, sir, I do." He nodded, "Then, you do understand, what, it is, I

expect from you? Disciplined study." I nodded.

"Mr. Will ...." He raised his head and scowled, "See to it, Mr. Peaster." I humbly yielded to my employer and he was gone. Not one to be argued with, I concluded. I set about getting myself cleaned up and unpacking my things. By two o'clock I was exhausted and collapsed on the bed, I was asleep before I was barely covered.

The clock chimed six and I reluctantly rose. Dressing and checking outside, it was clear as a bell with stars shining. I put on my coat and headed towards the house. On approaching, the windows were glowing warmly with lamplight. It didn't feel as intimidating compared to this afternoon. I happened to look up and saw someone standing on the balcony. "Good evening." I greeted the figure with a wave but it was still. I didn't recall seeing any statues and felt silly. Then, with one step, the figure was inside and the door was closing.

I stood there for a moment, perturbed, trying to see any shadows moving about, I relented and went to the front door. A tall, gaunt man opened the door before I could knock. "Good evening, sir." I nodded, "I'm Mr. Peaster." He let me in and I handed him my coat. "Yes, sir, my name is Peeler, I was to meet you tonight, afterwards you may let yourself in for meals. Breakfast is at six, dinner at one, and of course supper at seven." I smiled at him, "Thank you, Peeler, I'll remember." He suspiciously eyed me, "This way, please."

The dining table was glowing with candlelight and the china and crystal gleamed. "Good evening, Mr. Will." He stood at the fire place stoking the logs, replacing the poker, he turned to me. I was astonished at the transformation. His hair and beard smooth and appropriate attire turned him into a rather dashing gentleman. It was his gaze that let you know he was a force to be reckoned with. "Ah. Mr. Peaster, I hope you are in better spirits?" He smiled. "Yes, thank you, a nap does wonders." He called out then, "Reginal, Phillip! Come to supper." The kitchen door opened and two boys, which I already knew were thirteen, slowly entered.

They stopped in front of Mr. Will and locked their gazes on me. I had to smile, although they were dressed alike in fashionable suits, they were two of the ugliest children I had ever seen. I greeted them and they bowed and said in unison they were pleased to make my acquaintance. I smiled at Mr. Will. "You look like intelligent boys. I know we will get along swimmingly." They bowed again remained staring at me with loathsome expressions. Mr. Will told them to sit, they obeyed and didn't speak the rest of the evening.

Dinner was excellent. I was introduced to Peeler's wife, Ida. She was also the cook, I praised her abilities, which made her blush. Afterwards, the boys were excused and Mr. Will told me he had an appointment. "I know you will probably like to plan you lessons for tomorrow and get some rest, I bid you goodnight." With that he was gone. I wanted to see the school house and Peeler provided a lamp for me.

Entering the single room I saw that there was a generous desk in front of a slate board, Maps of the world adorned the walls, text books were neatly stacked on the desk, and a large dictionary stood in the corner on its own stand. Two rows of four desks filled the room. It was outfitted very nicely. At the back stood a wood stove with an ample supply of wood. I felt better about the entire situation. Now I shall plan my lessons and go to bed.

December 8, 1916

This week, went well. The twins are very intelligent and answer my questions with authority. They are quiet and do their school work. I noticed that they never engage with the other children during recess and dinner, they sit by themselves away from the others. The other children who are attending are Francis, who is twelve, her brother Toby, eleven years of age and little Freddie, six. He is their cousin. They were very timid the first day but have relaxed and are enjoying their studies. Francis is very bright and helps the boys a great deal. Toby informed me that he was the one who filled the wood boxes. I thanked him for a well done job. He smiled proudly. I need to dress for supper. I've been letting myself in the kitchen door and pass the time with Ida until it is time to serve. Must go.

December 15, 1916

It is getting closer to Christmas and while the other children are *delighting in decorating the school house, Reginal and Phillip are im-mersed in their books. I tried to persuade them to join but they refuse. I waited for them to be excused from the table last night and asked Mr. Will about the situation. "Don't wonder about my boys, Mr. Peaster. Let the other children have their fun. They will have to learn that the world doesn't revolve around them. Don't misunderstand, Mr. Peaster, they do know their Bible, we merely do not indulge in all the festivi-ties."*

I bowed to him, understanding. "By the way, Mr. Peaster, do you have plans, since school will be closed, what will you do?" I thought about it and shrugged, "I suppose I'll find some way to amuse myself, I may go into town and have a look about." He smiled. "Yes, I sup-pose they will have something going on to amuse you." He paused, "I suppose you have no family to visit." I shook my head, "No. Sir."

"Well, Mr. Peaster, I have an appointment, good night." I wished him a good night and sat there for a moment until I was interrupted by Ida who wanted to clear the table. I followed her into the kitchen and Peeler asked me if I would like to join them at their daughter's home for the holidays. "We have a new grand daughter." Ida gushed triumphantly. "We're so excited to see her. Do join us." I thought how nice it would be to visit a cheery home for a change and accepted.

January 6, 1917

School is back in session and everyone has settled down. Francis, Toby and Freddie had given me a new neck tie before school let out. I hugged them and thanked them, they beamed with pride as I replaced it for the one I was wearing. I caught the twins expressions out of the corner of my eye. The way they glared at our little group was unnerv-ing, their envy was quite apparent, I felt sorry for them. The scorn left their faces when Francis gave each of them a candy cane. They were gracious accepting them and wishing her a merry Christmas, I was amazed.

My three, as I've come to call them, skipped out the door joying in the presents I gave them, a silver dollar each. The twins took their time getting their things together. "Do you have any plans for your long weekend." I asked. They looked at one another. "We'll probably go out of town with father." Reginal replied. I was wiping down the board, "Oh! And where would you be going?" There was no answer and when I turned they were gone. What on earth, was going on in their little lives, that make them, act so, strangely?

My time, spent with Ida and Peeler, at their daughter's home was, delightful. Their daughter, Rachel, and her husband, William, were gracious hosts. Their home was warm and cozy. The new baby, Elizabeth, looked like an angel. Ida, cooed over her the entire time as Peeler strutted around, very proud of his family. I noticed the entire time that no word was ever spoken about Mr. Will. I assumed, they didn't want to put a damper on the merriment that would be over, too soon.

Alas, it is over. On the train back to Pierce, I listened while Ida planned out how they could all visit often because Mr. Will goes out of town so frequently. "Does he always take the boys?" I asked. Ida nodded, "Yes, every time." "What about their school work?" I ventured. Ida snorted. Peeler, patted her hand. She gave him a defiant look.

"I don't understand something, don't they have a mother?" They both looked at me with great eyes. "I only mention it, because I remember my first night at the house as I was walking up, I swear I saw someone standing on the balcony." I leaned back in my seat. "It didn't move making me think it was a statue but then I saw it go back inside." They stared at me for some time and Peeler grasped Ida's hand. "No, Mr. Peaster, you didn't see a statue, that was Emily Will." Ida spoke gravely.

"She's not in the best of health. Mr. Will has had to take over raising Reginal and Phillip." Peeler added.

"Who is taking care of her, while everyone is away." I snapped. They both jumped, "Don't worry yourself, Mr. Peaster, she's taken care of." Somehow, I didn't believe that. "Who takes care of her, I didn't see anyone arrive before we left." Peeler spoke with authority. "There are some things that are not your business, Mr. Peaster." His expression was very serious and I thought it best to let the matter drop. We left the train in silence as well as the ride to the house. I tried *apologizing, they accepted, reluctantly. I left to go to my own cottage and unpack.*

February 9, 1917

Supper at the Will home has been very quiet these last few weeks. Mr. Will is civil only not as genial. I wondered if I was out of the way concerning Mrs. Will. I pondered if I should explain or let things pass. I thought it best to let it pass. If Mr. Will wanted to say something, he would.

March 1, 1917

Today, I felt bold and thought I would ask the twins how their mother was faring. They only looked, at one another and went back to their lessons. I didn't pursue the matter. This evening at dinner, Mr. Will excused them from the table and said he wanted a word with me. I felt a wave of nausea sweep over me. The look on his face actually frightened me. "Mr. Peaster, when I hired you it was to have you here in the position of teacher. That is all. I don't want my staff or my children waylaid with a lot of questions that are no one's business. You are my employee, I invite you into my house, merely as a guest. Do not become so comfortable to think you can nose about in my affairs."

I began to speak, he continued. "You may continue to take your meals with us, I'll have no more of you harassing my family." I nodded. "If it is one thing I cannot abide, Mr. Peaster, it is hiring someone to do a job, such as teaching my boys, taking my money and doing that job so poorly." The fear I felt was rattling, I stammered my answer. "I do apologize, Mr. Will, I was naturally concerned. I have stepped over the boundaries and it will not happen again."

His hateful eyes reminded me our first day when he confronted poor Kranston. "So be it. We'll see you at breakfast. Goodnight." He stormed out of the room I collapsed back in my chair. A hot tear rolled down my cheek, I wiped it away quickly when Ida came in to clear the dishes. She didn't say a word or look at me. I waited until she left before I walked home.

Standing on the front porch I took a deep breath and collected myself. It was a clear night and cold. I was about to step down when I heard voices above me. I sneaked around carefully so I wouldn't be seen to see who it was. I knew Mr. Will's voice right away the other was barely audible. "Don't try and get smart with me, Emily. I know you've been watching him." I strained to hear what Mrs. Will was saying but it was no use.

"Father doesn't like snoops." I spun around to see Reginal and Philip standing there. For the first time since I had known them, they smiled. It was the most sickening thing I'd ever seen. I couldn't speak and couldn't think of anything to say, if I could. They merely turned and went back the way they came. I took the chance to look above me in case they were heard, not seeing anyone, I ran as fast as I could to my cottage.

March 9, 1917

I haven't been sleeping very well these last few nights. It is showing during the day. I actually snapped at poor little Freddie and he began crying. I felt like an ogre and apologized immediately. I gave him a peppermint and patted his head, he was immediately gratified. I felt, so tired after I excused the class I went straight home and collapsed in bed. I must've been to tired to dream for I awoke feeling better than I had in awhile.

On my way to breakfast I happened to glance up to the balcony. Actually, now, it was on purpose, to try and see if Mrs. Will would be outside. This morning I saw her standing at the door with the curtain pulled aside. I couldn't make out her features but I was rewarded with a wave. I waved back before I could stop myself. What if I were seen? It would only be more trouble for her as well as, myself.

With breakfast over I headed towards school. I heard a crash from behind. I spun about to look and saw that the glass panes of her balcony door had been shattered. I felt terrible, someone did see. I had to begin class and walked on.

April 6. 1917

We are at war. So many of the men in town have enlisted. It is very upsetting for all. I myself wasn't able to enlist as I am past the age limit. Mr. Will, also is past the age requirement, at least that is what he said. The war doesn't seem to bother him, in the least.

December 27, 1917

So it went these many months. I stayed out of Mr. Will's business and kept to myself. I taught my class and had my meals. This Christmas I wasn't invited to go with Ida and Peeler to their daughter's home. We haven't been on speaking terms since. I go into town once in a great while and have a meal at a café, if only, to be away from, the monotony of, Mr. Will's, household. I try to strike up conversations with a few, of the towns people while waiting on my meal. They will acknowledge my presence with a reciprocating remark concerning the weather but they turn their attention to someone else and I am left alone.

I have thought of leaving, but where would I go. I have a safe haven here where nobody knows me or my past. I am so very much a prisoner and when I think of it, it is my own doing. The children are doing very well. My three are thriving. All have had their birthdays and are growing in their bodies and minds. Francis will be a heartbreaker when she is grown. Toby will be a handsome man, and little Freddie will, I hope, be as kind and gentle, as he is now.

Of course the twins, Reginal, who is the more dominant, and Phillip haven't changed. They grow taller as well does their hateful attitude, unfortunately, they are as ugly as when I first met them. I usually spend my time reading and for some reason when I make my way to the house I still look up to the second floor wondering if I'll catch a glimpse of Mrs. Will. Since that morning when the glass was broken nothing was ever spoken of the situation. The glass was replaced and she hasn't ventured toward it.

June 6, 1918

There hasn't been anything to report, except that I was informed by Mr. Will that Mrs. Will has been sent to a sanitarium for her nerves. Poor woman, my heart goes out to her. My life is as dull as ever. *Everyday the same thing happens. The children are the only bright spot in my life now. They grow and grow and excel in their studies. I am so used to the twins it has become a bit of sport for me to put them on the spot when something funny has been said and my three laugh but not them. I make it a point to ask them why they did not find it humorous, they only glare at me and sit back in their chairs. I let it go and move on with the day. I don't do it all the time but some reaction from them is better than nothing.*

November 11, 1918

It is a time of rejoicing as the war has ended. I feel for all the families, those whose men are coming home and those that aren't. Most of the town is celebrating. I sat at the café and watched the festivities.

January 24, 1919

It was an interesting morning. Mr Will has returned from one of his jaunts. I was sitting at breakfast, reading the paper, when he strode in. "Good morning, Mr. Peaster." He was in a good mood, it was, unnerving. "Good morning, sir." He piled his plate high and took a seat next to me. I folded my paper and thought I should leave. "Stay, Mr. Peaster, I have something to talk to you about." Oh no, I thought, what did I do now.

"I've been neglecting you.' He smiled. 'No one can live the way you do and like it. I think you need to have some fun. You're still a young man." I didn't know what to say. "I go into town once in awhile." He looked at me weirdly. "And, do, what? Sit, in dreary cafe's, talking, to the locals? Or, go see the plays the ladies club performs in thinking they have talent?" I hated to admit it but I nodded that was exactly what I did.

No more. I haven't shown you all the sights this place has to offer. Tomorrow night,' he crammed the last fork full of food in his mouth and sat the plate down. 'Be ready to go after supper." He left just as hurried as he entered. I couldn't imagine what he had planned. At my desk, my eyes drifted over the class as they were working on their math test. I smiled seeing little Freddie softly counting with his fingers.

I rested my gaze on the twins. They are tall and gangly and still ugly. They were sixteen. They, had not passed, that awkward stage, they latched onto it. I looked past them to where Francis was sitting. She, was concentrating on a problem, when she happened to glance up and caught me looking at her. She smiled. I gave her a stern look and she went back to her reading. She is almost fifteen now and her beauty is more apparent. She has a lovely figure and in a few years she would be stunning. I felt I was being watched and saw that Toby was looking at me looking at Francis. I cleared my throat and called that the test was over. Little Freddie groaned and put his pencil down. Francis gathered the papers and brought them to me.

When school let out I cleaned the board and went to my cottage to change. It was a Friday so I could enjoy myself tonight without worrying about school the next day. It was cold out so I brought my heavy coat with me. Hopefully, I wouldn't get mud slung on me with Mr. Will driving the carriage.

January 26, 1919

The world is crashing down around me. I feel so sick I want to die. I'm ashamed of myself and what I have done. I thought coming here would be a new beginning, but my old ways have returned and I fear I won't be able to stop. I keep hearing Mr. Will's mocking me, "All work and no play, Mr. Peaster."

After dinner we climbed into the carriage and of course he took off like a wild man. I hung on for dear life until he slowed the horses as we entered Pierce proper. Once past the town, he picked up pace again, at least it wasn't raining. Too soon, we were leaving town and turning onto a narrow road. Exactly, where was he taking me? We must've driven another mile when I saw lights peeking thru the trees.

Coming to a clearing, there stood a large, two, story, house. Lights were on in every window and the closer we came you could hear music and laughter. A teenage boy ran up to the carriage and Mr. Will threw him the reins as he descended. "Take care of them, Darby." He said. Darby led them away. I was smoothing my hair down when Mr. Will walked over to me. "What is this place?" I asked, taking it all in.

He smirked derisively, " I think you know, Mr. Peaster, nevertheless, it's known as Lettie's. Lettie is the proprietress. " He winked.

I followed him up the steps and the large french doors were opened, immediately. I stood in the foyer searching around. Typically, red paint covered every wall, couches and chairs with velvet cushions were scattered about. Girls of every shape, size and age paraded back and forth in their frilly corsets and bloomers. Some wore faded night gowns that were barely hanging on. Some smiled as they passed by others merely looked bored. An older woman took our coats and hats. I began to ask Mr. Will something only he had walked further into the parlor.

I followed and caught up with him sitting at a table with a girl already in his lap, Darby waited for his order. "Sit down, Mr. Peaster, relax." I complied but I wasn't relaxed. He instructed Darby to bring his bottle and two glasses. The girl in his lap cooed, "I don't get any?" He silenced her with a kiss then he turned his attention to me. "What do you think, Mr. Peaster, you like it?"

I was nervous about the whole situation. "Really, Mr. Will, I don't think that someone in my position should be here." I was shocked when he stood up so vehemently, forcing the girl to fall to the floor. "Your position!" He snarled. I felt like fleeing, I know my eyes were as big as twin moons. Everyone around us stopped what they were doing to gawk at the upset. "How is your position anymore important than mine!"

"Mr. Will, I meant no disrespect to you or.." My words fell on deaf ears as he helped the girl back onto his lap, rubbing her bottom. Darby returned with a large crystal decanter and two glasses, setting them down he looked to Mr. Will who nodded. He proceeded to pour out the colorful liquid and left us. Mr. Will sat a glass in front of me and raised his own in a toast. "I don't often say this to many people, but I like you, Mr. Peaster. Here is to your second anniversary in my employ. I hope you last longer than Mr. Collins." He clinked my glass and swallowed it down at once. Mr. Collins, there was that name again. I wanted to ask exactly what happened to Mr. Collins but his glaring eyes changed my mind.

I could smell the heady mixture and expecting the worst, I braced myself, and took a sip. It was sweeter than I expected. Not to insult him, I swallowed the rest, as he had. Letting out a cough, I sat the glass down and waited for the burning sensation to cease. He was smiling at me and filled the glasses again, remarking, 'that's fine.' He immediately finished his glass and kissed the girl on his lap while fondling her ample breast.

When I sat my glass down I noticed it didn't burn as before and the sweetness took over. I craved another and said so, Mr. Will happily complied. "Good, Mr. Peaster, enjoy, you've been cooped up far too long. " I picked up the glass and saluted him. I remember him saying 'we'll see how you feel about your position, tomorrow.' I wanted to say something but was interrupted by the loveliest girl I'd ever known, standing in front of me. She dipped her finger into my glass and brought it to her lips smearing the liquid across her tender mouth, then she bent down and lightly kissed me. The last thing I remember was following her down a hallway.

Upon waking that afternoon, my eyelids were of lead, my head full of wet sand and my stomach was on fire. All made worse when I tried to sit up. I tried to focus my eyes, the only light peeked around the edges of the curtains. I lay back and rolled over into a warm body, reeling back, I tried to remember what had happened and soon gave up. Painfully, I stood and made my way to the window. Pulling the curtain back, was as excruciating as I thought it would be. Bending down for my clothes that were strewn about was a herculean effort.

I sat on the edge of the bed and looked around to the girl who was stirring. Her face peeked above the covers staring at me as I struggled into my trousers. Her cry of pain made me cringe when she sat up. I forced myself to face her. Looking at her now with most of her make up rubbed off I saw how young she really was. "Are you alright?" I croaked. "Yeah, they told me I would be sore." I squeezed my eyes shut at the thought. She crawled out from under the covers and reached for her gown. Raising it over her head, it fell down the length of her perfect body. I became aroused, she left the room before I could act.

Just as well, I thought. Unable to find my tie I pulled the covers back to see if it had ended up on the bed. What I saw was a small stain of blood, the room began spinning and I was soaked with sweat. I wretched into the wash bowl on the stand. I soaked a towel in the water pitcher and washed myself down. I felt cooler and the room stopped spinning. I didn't care what I had left behind, I headed for the door, immediately.

Reaching the foyer, I was almost free when Mr. Will called out. Nausea washed over me when he mentioned food. I slowly walked to his table. It was very quiet in the house. The grin on Mr. Will's face should have bothered me, I was too sick to care. He pushed a cup of coffee over to me, I couldn't look at it. He chuckled, "Maybe, you need a little hair of the dog. I can order-" I interrupted, "No, no, no thank you. "

"What is wrong, Mr. Peaster, you seem unusually upset?" I squinted my eyes at him, dumbfounded by his comment. "I don't remember what happened last night and this afternoon I find blood on the sheet. It's terrible what I did to that poor girl."

"Don't feel bad, Mr. Peaster, she had to be broke in by somebody." I looked at him in disgust. "You didn't have to pay this time but you will the next, and believe me it won't cost you as much as it did me." I tried to stand up but my throbbing head forced me to sit. "What are you talking about." I whispered. He chuckled. "You know as well as I do that deflowering a virgin is a lot more expensive than what you pay for a-"

"You can't be serious, there isn't going to be a next time." With that he guffawed loudly making my ears ring. "I don't think it is a laughable situation, Mr. Will." He sobered from his laughter. "Well, you weren't laughing at the merchandise, last night. She was alright, wasn't she just about the age you like and all?"

"What?" I spoke in horror. " I said you like them at that age, isn't that right, Mr. Peaster?"

I know I was crying then but all I could do was sit there and listen. "You were pretty good for a long time. I wondered how long it would take. Then I was walking by the school one day, and I noticed you were most intent watching little Francis playing in the yard. She's a beautiful little girl, I have to admit, but she's off limits. Did you think it was a fluke that I contacted you for a teaching position? I travel about and I talk to a lot of people and your name came up more than once in different towns.

Always the stories were the same. You would talk your way into some financially comfortable household, usually, charming the mother's who in turn would charm the father's into thinking that was exactly what they needed so their children would have better educations. At least that's the story the mother's tried to sell. They knew that affording a tutor showed how prosperous they were and how jealous their friends would be who couldn't afford one.

You would stay for awhile if they only had boys then you'd find some excuse to leave but if they had a daughter, my, my, my Mr. Peaster. You would do everything in your power to let that girl think you and she were meant to be. You would use her as long as possible until you were found out or you got sick of her, then you moved on.

I wiped at my eyes, "I changed. I stopped myself. I wanted to quit running and live a normal life." He leaned back. "A leopard can't change his spots, Mr. Peaster. Now, whenever Francis rouses any desires in you, you can come here and take care of things." I felt depleted and stood to leave. "Tell me, Mr. Will, why?" He stood up and put his coat on. "I told you last night, I like you. No reason throwing away a perfectly good teacher because of one little flaw." I rubbed my head. "I assure you, I won't be back." He stood before me. "Don't be silly, of course, you will."

He offered to take me home, I knew I couldn't stand his driving and declined. "If you feel like walking I'll let you in on a little secret." I was listening.. "This town is built, if you notice, in the shape of a horse shoe. My house sits by the river and so does this place. If you follow the river you'll find a grove of trees, walk straight thru those and you'll be home in no time." I was stunned. "Why the long drive last night, then?' He took the reins in his hands. "Mr. Peaster, you don't need to know everything." He smiled and slapped the reins.

The cool air felt good on my face and I began walking in the direction of the river. I could see the barges and river boats sailing away. I kept at a slow pace, taking it all in. My headache was subsiding but my thirst was great, I knelt by a low spot on the bank and drank the cold water. I must've swallowed to much as I immediately wretched it up. I rolled onto my back on the cold ground and shut my eyes. I don't know how long I stayed there when a horn from one of the boats sounding jolted me awake. The sun was waning, I hurried on my way.

Lying on the cold ground didn't help my already aching body. The earth was becoming more uneven and every jolting step caused my head ache to return. I found the woods and became worried as what little light there was faded fast the further I went. More than once I would trip over something that sent me sprawling. I knew, that my face and hands were bleeding from all the limbs and thorns slapping at me. I couldn't see anything at one point and very slowly I felt for the trees to guide me.

Soon, I was able to make out dim lights ahead. They were from the main house, I felt relief at the sight of my beacon. I managed to step into two deep trenches before I was able to make the clearing. I deducted that I had walked no more than a mile, but in my state it felt like a hundred. I entered my cottage and made it to bed before passing out. When I awoke it was day break.

February 2, 1919

It has been a week since my episode at Lettie's and I find it very difficult to stay away. He is relentless when supper is over, always inviting me to join him. It has become annoying and I usually beg off with some excuse concerning lessons. He only gives me a mocking smile and leaves. He won't get the better of me. I can change. Never again.

February 23, 1919

I have spent quite a lot of time at Lettie's. I loathe my weakness yet Mr. Will was right. I see Francis and begin to think, I can not do that to her. Not because of Mr. Will telling me she was off limits, she is very special and doesn't need me ruining her life. Mr. Will has a bottle set aside for me when he is unable to accompany me, I fear I frequent the place more often than he.

August 15,1919

All the money that I managed to save for two years is gone. Lettie won't give me any credit and Mr. Will won't advance my salary. "You should be more careful, Mr. Peaster. I thought you could regulate yourself better than that." He mocked me. "Luckily, you'll be paid before school begins." I felt slighted by that remark. He always had to make some gesture concerning Francis.

He then informed me that he would be away with the twins for three weeks. "Find some way to amuse yourself, Mr. Peaster." He laughed as he left the dining room. I was fostering a deep resentment towards his arrogance. Always, laughing at my weaknesses. I relished the thought of finding a way to knock him down a peg. How? That was the problem. I needed to find out something about him. He seemed to know all about me.

August 16, 1919

I watched out the dining room window as Mr. Will and the twins drove out of sight. Ida, was washing up the last of the breakfast dishes before she and Peeler headed for their daughter's home. Even tho we weren't as close as I hoped, she still informed me how well her family was and even went so far to tell me that another baby was on the way. I congratulated her and she smiled. Peeler, beckoned her that they would miss the train and she said goodbye. I watched out the dining room window and they disappeared down the drive.

I lingered at the table with my cup of coffee, promising I would wash it and put it away. I sat at the dining table and looked around the room. It was strange, I thought, that I had never really looked at this house. I knew that the table and chairs were the finest available as were the candlesticks and dishware but I had never noticed the things in a house that made it a home. It was clear to me now that there was nothing to look at.

There was no display of extravagance anywhere. Most homes I had inhabited usually made it a point to have their riches around them. There was no mantle adorned with candles only the hardware needed to stoke a fire sat on the cold slab in the corner. An utter lack of decor abounded. I ambled into the front room. There were two chairs and a sofa with two side tables and two small lamps sitting on top all alone.

The walls were bare, no portraits, pictures or tapestries of any kind. No rugs on the floor only what was needed to let you know that this was where you could sit, if they had any visitors, that is. Plain heavy curtains dressed the windows. I felt a chill as I stood in the huge room. I imagined it with the fireplace roaring, a grand piano in one corner, a portrait of Mr. Will gracing one wall, a nice mirror on another. Pictures of the twins as they grew, scattered about.   Plush pillows to rest upon and beautiful rugs to help, keep the cold off of your feet. This place looked as if it were vacant and someone would come soon to get the last few items. Had Mrs. Will been an invalid all her life, where was that woman's touch.

I found another room off the main, which must be Mr. Will's office, it contained a desk, similar to mine, a chair and three file cabinets. I noticed none of them were labeled. I tried every drawer, naturally, they were locked. The thought of breaking the locks entered my mind which I quickly disregarded. The three top desk drawers were not locked, unlike the bottom two on either side. I lifted the contents carefully finding what appeared to be an address book.

Flipping each page I found a number of addresses which meant nothing to me, I decided to copy them down just the same. Who knows, I might need them in the future. I made sure that everything was just as I found it. I felt nervous being in his private office and left it forthwith. My curiosity, lead me up the large staircase. I turned left deciding to begin with that end of the house. The door at the end was ajar and I gently pushed it open.

It was a large room with two single beds in either corner. A dresser sat between the two windows. An armoire housed the remnants of the twins' suit's they always wore. There were no toys or any such things that boys might have. I laughed at calling them boys, they were *nearly grown now, and wouldn't have toys. Shouldn't they have, at least, something of a hobby? Most young men liked something. Model trains, stamp collecting, something. There was nothing. Except for their school books neatly stacked on their bedside tables.*

I pulled the door to, as I had found it and went to the next. It was shut but not locked. This room was massive. It should have had a magnificent, four poster, bed plunged in the middle, instead, a single bed, neatly made up, occupied the corner opposite the window. A chest, of drawers and another armoire were the only furnishings. I hoped it might be a guest room, I knew better. How could Mr. Will live in such meagerness?

I knew he was financially sound and yet, I was astonished. No wonder Ida could take care of this house, there was nothing to it. She wasn't inundated dusting every little trinket.

Fluffing, hundreds of pillows and washing great loads of laundry. I imagine it didn't bother her, in fact, the most she had to take care of, were their rooms. I had the chance to see them when we were still on speaking terms and she wanted to show off the new pictures of her grand baby. It was a cozy place, she had enough things crammed into their sitting room to outfit the main room. Portraits of her little family adorned every flat surface.

I opened each drawer of his and looked for anything that might aid me. Nothing, only neatly folded clothes and accessories. I felt like giving up and thought of the armoire. I opened the doors and found it empty with only a few hangers left dangling. There were two drawers on the bottom which had locks, I tried them and they opened. Inside were packets of letters, neatly bundled and bound with ribbon. I looked at some of the addresses alas they meant nothing to me.

My intention of reading them was put off when I thought I heard a noise. I quickly put them back and closed up the armoire. I listened for a moment, maybe it was my imagination, or maybe I made the noise myself, scraping against something, either way, it was quiet. I went softly to the door and listened, feeling sure there was nothing I quietly opened the door and stepped out.

Latching the door as I had found it, I was about to turn. "You have your nerve, Mr. Peaster." I let out a scream and jumped turning around to see who was behind me. "Oh my, oh my, I didn't mean to frighten you, please, I didn't mean to frighten you." It was a woman's voice but not Ida, the only woman in this house. Catching my breath I took in the sight before me. The woman standing there was tall in height wearing a white blouse with a gray and white striped skirt on a trim figure.

She held a walking cane in either hand. Her shocking white hair was pulled back in a loose bun with silver combs on either side. Her eyes held mine as she spoke, "It's alright, Mr. Peaster, don't be alarmed." I wish I could describe her face, only she didn't have one. A black veil covered her from below the eyes to her chin which was drawn taunt by two ribbons.

My breathing calmed as I was mesmerized by her kindly eyes. They were a brilliant color of green. "That's better,' she said. 'I'm sorry to have given you such a scare." I took a step back and straightened up. "My apologies, but who are you?" She hung her cane on her left arm and held out her hand. "Very pleased to meet you, I am Emily Will." I grasped her hand without thinking then pulled back swiftly. "I don't understand, when did you return?"

"Return! I've been here all along. May I call you Daniel, I hate formalities?" I must have nodded for she said 'Good, call me Emily." She told me to follow her and I did. We walked to the end of the hall. It was a slow pace since she was not able to take very large steps. It was painful to hear her labored breathing as she moved. I followed her into her room. It was smaller than the others and only furnished with a chaise lounge and two chairs with a small table in between. She had a few pillows about and a cabinet with a brandy decanter and glasses sitting on a silver tray.

She hobbled to the chaise and sat down pushing herself back and with both hands she gathered her skirt tightly and lifted her legs over the side to rest on the cushion. "That's better. If you would be so kind as to pour us a couple of brandies. I could use one and I'm sure you could after your fright." I did as she requested. I handed her a glass and she reached back and pulled the bottom ribbon of her veil. Simultaneously lifting the veil and the glass so as not to reveal anything and took a healthy sip. "Very fine." I sampled mine, which it was, very fine brandy.

"I apologize for my behavior, I thought I was alone."

"Obviously."

"You don't understand, I was under the impression you were in a sanitarium." She laughed at that. "He wishes I were." She sipped again. "Don't be so nervous Daniel." I guess I was fidgeting again. "I really shouldn't be here."

"Nonsense."

"I don't think Mr. Will would like it if he found out."

"Then don't tell him. I won't." I eyed her suspiciously. She seemed nonchalant, I couldn't help thinking I was making a mistake. "So, Daniel, what are your plans?" I didn't understand her meaning. "For the future."

"Teaching my pupils, I suppose."

"The boys will be off to college soon, then what?"

"Well, there are the other three and maybe more will join in time." She snickered. "Don't mind me, Daniel, please." I did not care for her attitude, I assumed she was nervous as well.

"How do you like it here?"

"I like it very much." I sipped my brandy. "Do you? Thomas tells me everything, you know, I know how he treats you. He's a very insulting man." Her tone sounded sincere. "I, suppose, so." I said.

"What are you doing upstairs?"

"Nothing. I was intrigued by the architecture downstairs and wandered up here." She nodded. "And what do you think?"

"It is very unpretentious." She laughed then. "Is that a fancy word for empty as a tomb?"

I didn't know what to say. "You must have thought the architecture included the filing cabinets and the armoire." I sobered then. "Keep in mind, Daniel, this house is empty and you were making enough noise that it echoed up here. That's how I knew you were here. I had just seen you go into Thomas' room when I looked down the hall.

I began to feel ill. She would tell him and that would be the end of it. She was his wife after all, she was probably as crazy as he. "Have another brandy, Daniel. You look flushed." I could only sit there, feeling trapped. "What were you hoping to find, Daniel?" I wiped a tear from my eye. "I believe I shall go?" She sat up straight. "Please, don't. I'm sorry, I shouldn't have said that." I stood to leave. "I know you want out, I can help you." I looked at her. How could she help, to seal my doom?

"I know you don't think you can trust me." I shook my head, "It is difficult, to know who to trust." She relaxed against the pillow. "You should go, now. Think it over. There will be plenty more times that we can talk." I gazed at her, her eyes were moist. Was she, sincere or insane? Only time would tell. I told her I would think about it and bade her good day.

I ran the entire way to my cottage. I wanted to pack up everything and leave but as I said I had no money. I never felt so helpless. Sitting here now, having had time to calm down and think, I feel terrible having acted in such a manner. I imagine she is very lonely. I wanted to scream at my predicament. She said she would help me, she said Mr. Will told her everything. Did she tell him everything as well. Terrible thoughts ran thru my mind. Was this a ploy to trap me. This is to much. I can not concentrate anymore.

September 5, 1919

I did not go back to see Emily the rest of the time. I kept myself busy, tidying my cottage and the school house. I planned out this year's curriculum, raising the standard of difficulty. I was getting dressed late this morning when I heard an unusual sound. Stepping outside I listened as it grew. Soon an automobile turned into the drive. I could see it was Mr. Will.

Intrigued, I hurried to follow. I met up with him as he and the twins were digging their suitcases out of the back. "This is impressive, Mr. Will, my compliments." He smiled at me. "Thank you, Mr. Peaster. I'll miss my horses but when I saw this I couldn't take my eyes off it."

"What make of auto mobile is this."

"A Cadillac."

"The twins ambled into the house and closed the door. "They look as if they enjoyed the ride." I spoke facetiously. Mr. Will paused looking at me strangely then broke into laughter. "Allow me to take you to lunch Mr. Peaster." Trepidation gripped me remembering being at his mercy while driving. Nevertheless, off we went. He was more careful around the turns with his new car, still, I was hanging on for dear life. Everyone in town turned to look at the impressive auto or maybe it was the surprise that Mr. Will decided to take advantage of a piece of modern machinery.

The café was fairly empty when we sat down, I noticed what few patrons there were, quickly paid their tabs and left. Mr. Will did not seem to notice. All thru lunch he spoke of how his car handled, the size of the engine and miles per gallon. I asked him why he decided on a car, he replied that he was tired of being at the mercy of the train schedule. I had never seen him act to happy, like a child with a new toy. I asked him what he had done with the horses.

"Sent them to the glue works." I was stunned. "Those beautiful horses."

"I don't need them anymore. Why? Did you want one of them?"

"Yes, actually. It is a long walk into town and back, especially if I have purchases."

"Not a problem, Mr. Peaster. We'll go over to Kitchens livery. I'm sure he has a horse for you." With that he handed me my salary. Dropping me off, Mr. Kitchens showed me around and I chose a horse. After haggling over price, I rode out with my four year old horse and a ten year old saddle. New harness and bridle. It was awkward at first, since I had not ridden in years. Soon, it all came back to me and once past town I galloped back to my cottage.

Mr. Will told me I could use the stables and the hay and feed that were left, which was ample. I brushed her down, decided to call her Millie, and gave her fresh water and feed. I felt calm, somehow, now that I had some mode of transportation. I counted what money I had left, although, tomorrow is the beginning of school I decided to go to Lettie's.

October 9, 1919

It has been well over a month since my encounter with Emily. I have been dreading the

day when he will bring up my being in the house. So far, he has not mentioned it by word or deed. Is he really none the wiser. I feel I may relax. I feel I was to quick to judge Emily. She said she would help me. I hope I will not need her help.

October 12, 1919

I was awakened by an awful scratching sound. My first thought was the wind blowing the tree branches against the roof, yet as I laid there listening I realized it wasn't overhead but lower. I crept over to the window to peek out. Possibly an animal scratching about, I couldn't see. I went to the next window and the scratching sound moved around the side. Every window I peered thru caused the sound to move further ahead. A complete turn around the house and it was at my door.

I was curious what it could be, I thought of what I might use for a weapon. Nothing came to mind, I thought it best to not open the door. It scratched around for the longest time. I went back to bed and tried to ignore it, even covering my head with my pillow, nothing helped. It wasn't until the sun began to dawn that the scratching ceased. I cursed whatever it was and sat up. I had to go to school. I checked every window again and then carefully opened the door and peeked out. Nothing was out there and I inspected the door for damage.

It appeared to be claw marks although unusual. I traipsed around the cottage and there were marks all around about four feet up. Strange I could not see it out the window. The marks on the house were not deep, the door took most of it since it went on forever. I will ask Mr. Will what he knows about the wild life around here.

Afternoon:

Mr. Will said he had never seen any critters around that could or would do something like

that. He walked around the cottage himself. "Unusual, Mr. Peaster, could possibly be a hungry dog. I'll keep an eye out, be careful." I thanked him and decided to put some food out in case it decided to come back. I had to sleep, hopefully it would eat and leave.

October 13, 1919

No scratching last night. The food was not touched. Odd. Whatever it was must have moved on. I hope this rain will stop by Friday.

October 29, 1919

Dr. Conroy removed my stitches this morning. I have been ill since the seventeenth. Ill, really is not the word, mortified, since the seventeenth, is more like it. I cannot stop thinking what happened. I was returning from Lettie's late Friday night and felt fine. Unfortunately, the rain continued and the lightning, was bothering Millie. I tried to soothe her as best I could when a lightning bolt struck a tree just in front of us and she bolted. Losing my balance, I fell off and she was gone. I made it home, and thought I would look for her in the morning.

I checked the grounds and stables and asked Mr. Will if he had seen her. He had not. He did suggest that since she was use to the livery, it was possible that she went there. He offered me a ride into town which I greatly appreciated. Mr. Kitchens said he had not seen her and offered to sell me another. I did not have the money to be buying horses every time I turned around and graciously declined. On the way back Mr. Will drove out of his way to help me look for her. She seemed to have disappeared. Giving up we went home.

At supper, Mr. Will offered that he would drive me to Lettie's if I were going that way. I thanked him and we were off. He disappeared from view as soon as we entered. I, followed my usual routine. Four glasses, a pretty girl and upstairs. Around two o'clock I had, had enough and wanted to leave. Downstairs, there were a few people lingering about, Mr. Will couldn't be found. I did not want to disturb him, wherever he was. It was not raining so I left on foot as I had before so many times.

As luck would have it, the rain began. I was soaked and cold and halfway thru the woods. The rain, turned into soft drizzle. It was very quiet that night. I took a step and heard a twig snap. I froze because the sound came from behind me. I thought of that thing scratching at my door and tried not to panic. I took another step, all was quiet. I relaxed, just my imagination. I began walking and my heart quickened. Something was coming towards me.

I ran to make the clearing. I had only a few more yards, when I slipped and slid most of the way. I gained my feet and turned around. The clouds had passed and let the moon light shine. I tried in vain to see if anything was there. I was breathing so terribly I thought I might collapse. I looked to my right and there was my cottage. Too soon, another cloud passed in front of the moon light leaving me in the dark. The sound of the ground being trampled propelled me on.

I made for the door and slamming it shut with my back against it, I was pushed off balance by the force banging into it from outside. I screamed and sank to the floor pushing against the door with all my might. A second forceful hit rocked the hinges. I could not think what I would do if whatever it was managed to break in. I sat there waiting for the longest time. My throat was dry from breathing so hard. I forced myself to calm down and thought I should get up until out of the corner of my eye I caught sight of a shadow standing at the window.

I believe I remember shrieking, I know I passed out.

Welcomed, morning light was streaming in. Wearing my wet clothes all night had not helped. I was so stiff it took awhile for me to stand. Slowly, I peeled off my damp clothes and put on my robe. I made myself a cup of tea. Warmer, I dressed and had a light breakfast. Thoughts of all that occurred kept running thru my mind. I felt silly now, remembering. My imagination had gotten the better of me, was all. I checked my appearance in the mirror deciding to have another look for Millie. I opened the door and that was all I remember.

When I woke up a figure was sitting by my bed. I tried to focus swearing that it was the shadow I had seen at my window. I blinked several times until Mr. Will came into focus. "You're lucky to be alive, Mr. Peaster. How do you feel?" I pushed myself up feeling the throbbing in my head. I put my hands to my head and felt the heavy bandages. "What happened?"

"You were attacked. You didn't show up for school Monday and the children came looking for you. They found you lying on the ground and ran to get me. I went for the doctor. He had to use a lot of stitches. You've had a fever."

My head was spinning. "Monday? What day is it?"

"Friday." My head ached. "I have been out for a week." He nodded. "You don't recall anything that happened." I tried to think. "No, sir. I remember opening the door and that is all."

We were quiet for a moment. "I wonder if whatever was scratching at your door is what attacked you?"

"I don't know. I do remember something chasing me thru the woods and hitting the door." "Did you hear anything, did it sound like an animal?"

"No, now that you mention it, there was no sound like that of a growl or anything."

"I wonder. It could be someone who works the barges." I looked at him. "You haven't been fighting with anyone at Lettie's have you?" I was shocked. "No! Sir. In fact I do not speak to anyone except the boy who brings my drink and the girl I have chosen." He thought for a moment. "This is certainly strange. First someone snoops around in my house and now you are attacked."

My eyes widened. "Snoops around your house?" He shrugged at me. "When I arrived home before school began. That evening I was in my office doing paperwork." He paused. "It sounds silly, have you ever felt that someone has been in your things even if nothing seems out of place." I swallowed. "You believe someone was in your house?"

"I know you have access to the house and I trust that you wouldn't be so bold as to rummage around." He peered at me. "No, sir. As usual I finished my breakfast that morning, and came directly here." He placated me, "Not to worry, Mr. Peaster, I'm not accusing you. I'm only curious if you possibly saw someone up at the house?"

"No, sir. As you can see, your house is so far away and the trees block most of it." He turned to look out the window and nodded. "True enough."

"What about your office?"

"Oh yes, as I said, I was taking care of my correspondence, I opened my address book and I noticed that the marker wasn't in the same place I'd left it. That was my first clue. Later, as I was unpacking, I opened the doors of my armoire and saw that one of the drawers wasn't shut. It seems a packet of old letters was tilted up and the drawer couldn't be closed properly."

I was feeling ill by now. How could I have been so sloppy? He offered me a glass of water which I immediately choked on. He slapped me on the back until I recovered. "Thank you, Mr. Will." I gasped and lay back. "Was anything missing?"

"No. That's what I don't understand."

"Should we bring in the authorities?"

"No, Mr. Peaster. Not for something so trivial, at least to them. I mean nothing was taken and apparently no witnesses."

"Very unnerving."

"I should let you rest, Mr. Peaster. I'll check on you later. Do take care, should you hear anything."

"Thank you, Mr. Will. Hopefully, this has all been a fluke."

"Hopefully." He spoke quietly and left.

I sank down in my pillow and covered my eyes. He knows, he knows! Or does he. Did Emily tell him and now he is playing cat and mouse? It pained me to get out of bed, I had to make sure my copy was still hidden. I had made it halfway across the room when I stopped. He was watching, I thought. Somehow, I felt he was watching. I crept over to the window and peeked around the curtain. I saw him walking towards his house. I panicked. He should have been further away, by then. I waited until he disappeared from view. Did he look around for my copies while I was unconscious? Was he waiting for me to slip? Was he waiting for another chance to kill me?

November 17, 1919

I have recovered from my attack. My wounds have healed leaving pencil thin white scars. When I think of how bad they looked when the bandages were removed, I cringe. When I looked in the mirror this morning I noticed that the scar on my forehead resembled the letter 'T'. I chuckled at the thought that I was now marked. Sitting at my desk, this afternoon, I noticed the twins were staring at me in a peculiar manner, almost one of sympathy.

"Is there a problem, Reginal?" He did not blink. "You look like our mother." They returned to their studies. I wanted to cry. I look forward to Christmas break, everyone will be away and I can apologize to Emily. If she will still speak to me.

December 8, 1919

Nothing has happened out of the ordinary since my attack. Maybe it was Mr. Will's way of a warning.

December 17, 1919

They have all left. I want to run straight to the house, it is so late. I believe I will go in the morning.

December 18, 1919

It has been a long day. I had not realized how long I sat there listening to Emily until she ended it. This morning I softly rapped on her door. She bade me to enter. She was reclined on her chaise finishing her toast and coffee. "How are you, Daniel?" Her eyes were affectionate and the warm tone of her voice made me feel ashamed for running away from her. I knelt down by her, "Will, you forgive me, Emily. I should not have behaved as I had."

She stroked my hair. "You don't need to explain, Daniel. I know what happened to you." She softly touched my forehead, tracing the scars. I noticed the scars on her forehead, in the middle was one similar to mine in the shape of a 'T'. Her eyes smiled at me. "Looks like we're both, branded." I did not understand. "Pardon?" She pointed to her, 'T' and then mine. "Traitor." I grabbed both of her hands and kissed them. "Help me, Emily, please."

"What would you like to know?" I searched her face. "Anything, everything. I need to find something out about him so I can, I don't know, have some kind of leverage."

"You think that's the best way?" I let go of her hands and stood up. "I don't know, Emily. He seems to relish the fact that he knows all about me. If I had something on him."

"Then he might leave you alone and you could leave without fearing, repercussion."

"Yes! I am so sick of all the secrets and the fear he loves to spread."

"I hope you know what you're getting into, Daniel. If he were to find out." I knelt beside her. "I swear to you I will not breath a word until I find what I am looking for. I will, of course, discuss it with you, if you think my ideas have merit and I am able to confront him."

"You don't have to worry about me. He can't hurt me." I wanted so to ask her how she became so crippled, I think she knew what I was thinking. "I tell you what, pour, us both a brandy and I'll tell you everything I know." I smiled at her and hurried to do her bidding. I was settled in my chair and she had a sip of her brandy. "That's fine. To begin, when I was little more than a month old our parents died when our house caught on fire. Thomas managed to get me out in time, they weren't so fortunate.'

"I beg your pardon?"

"What is it?" I leaned in, "Your parents died in a fire?"

"Correct."

"Mr. Will was there."

"Right."

"His parents perished as well?"

"Of course, didn't I say it right. Our parents died in a house fire."

"I don't understand. Are you telling me that Mr. Will is your brother."

"Of course, silly."

"Brother!"Bizzle choked on his scotch. He laid the book down and sat on the edge of the chair with his head down. "Brother!" He choked out. "What the hell!" He recovered himself and picked the book up settling back.

"But– what is this Mrs. Will, nonsense." She laughed. "I'll come to that if you'll just hold your horses. "Now, the police picked us up and sent me to Mrs. Tuttle's home for girls. Since it was for girls only they

sent him to Claremont home for boys. The only reason I knew I had a brother was when I received a letter from him. I was almost eleven when it arrived. There was no return address only a postmark from somewhere in the Philippines.

I went up to my attic at the home to read it. Everybody else was afraid to go up there, it was my private retreat. I began reading, he warned me right away not to show the letter to anyone or to even talk about it. I thought it was silly but I never said a word, in a way I liked having it as a secret. He went on to say how he thought of me often. He knew I wouldn't remember him but to keep on the lookout, that he would be coming for me.

He boasted of how rich he was and how wonderful it will be when we are reunited. He told me that he would take care of me and buy me anything I wanted and that I should seriously consider what I wanted to do with my life. He was adamant that I have a college education so I would have a better chance in life. I was stunned, there I was rotting in that orphanage and I receive this packet of hope and promises.

He went on to tell me that he had ran away from his orphanage almost a year after arriving there. He said he hated being cooped up and having orders barked at him all the time. He especially despised one of the orderlies that worked there and he had to get out. He said he had ran all the way to the docks and managed to board a ship without being seen that was going to sea. He hid until he was discovered by a couple of the crew. They hauled him up and the captain decided they were too far out to turn around so he put him to work. There he stayed sailing the oceans. He described all the wonderful places where they had docked and how we would visit them together someday. I was walking on a cloud for the longest time.

She paused for another brandy. "What happened then?"

"Nothing. I didn't hear from him until almost four years later."

"Why so long?"

"I don't know. I actually met him in person the next time. I was in town taking care of some errands when I was approached by a very handsome young man. He called me by name and told me he was my

brother. I was happy and angry all at once. "You didn't write to me."
I said. He told me that he was back at sea and never had the chance
to write again. But he was here now and if I wanted to go with him.
Of course, I wanted to go with him, I was so miserable and now he
was there.

He asked when I would be in town again. I said I always did my
errands on Wednesdays but that I could leave right then. No, he said,
we can't let on that I'm here. Just wait until next week. Pack what I
could but not so much as to cause suspicion. I told him I didn't have
anything except another dress like the one I was wearing. He said he
needed time to arrange our trip and that the same time next week to
meet him at the train station. I begged to go with him then, that I
wouldn't cause any trouble but he made me promise to wait. I was
depressed but I did as he asked.

"He basically kidnaped you."

"I was willing. At the time I didn't care why he was acting the way
he was. He could have

come to the home and explained to Mrs. Tuttle the situation, as
I said, at the time, I didn't care. I wanted out and I was getting out.
The next Wednesday couldn't come fast enough, I didn't let on and
kept to my routine. As soon as I was out of sight of the home I ran as
fast as I could to the train station. There were quite a lot of people and
I searched all over for Thomas. I became frantic because I couldn't
find him.

The train sitting on the tracks when I arrived had pulled out. I
just knew I'd missed him. I sat on a bench and cried. Soon another
train pulled in and I watched for him. The porter called all aboard
and it started up. I was about to give up hope and stood to leave
when a hand grabbed my arm and pulled me toward the car. He had
been running he hoisted me onto the train and jumped in just as it
was gaining speed. The porter took our tickets and showed us to our
seats.

"Where were you?" I demanded to know. He said he had some last
minute business to attend and hadn't realized the time. He apolo-
gized for making me worry. After that we settled down and I asked

him about this house and what he did for a living. Now that we had time I wanted to get to know my brother."

I thought life was going to be grand. The first night when we arrived here I began to feel ill. The next morning, Thomas was knocking at my door to take me to breakfast, I couldn't answer I was in the bathroom. He rushed inside and found me sitting on the floor. I looked up at him and the most strange look came over him. It scared me quite frankly. He took me to the doctor in Colson and I found out I was pregnant. I lurched forward, "Oh no!" She patted my hand.

"Well, when we returned to the house he asked me who was responsible. I was so stupid about life, I didn't really understand what he was saying. He realized he was frightening me and calmed down. He tried, nervously, to explain what causes pregnancy. I wanted to cry as I realized what had happened. I told him what Chauncey had done."

"Who is Chauncey?"

"He was the hired man. He worked at the orphanage some times doing the heavy work. It seemed to me he spent a lot of his time watching the girls. All of us avoided him. It wasn't that he was only ugly, which he was, it was the way he leered at you. He was always trying to get one of the girls alone. He never tried with me until a couple of weeks before I met Thomas. I was up in my attic reading. He surprised me, he was so quiet. I warned him to get out, he only laughed. I fought as best as I could. When it was over, he just got up and walked away.

"Did you tell anyone?"

"Tell who?" I'd overheard a couple of the girls complain to Mrs. Tuttle, only to be told they were at fault for leading him on." I shook my head, "I'm so sorry, Emily." She gestured, "It's over and done with now. Thomas was beside himself, he sat in a chair in my room brooding, not speaking. I tried not to cry but I couldn't help it. I kept thinking what would happen to me now. What would he do?" I cried myself to sleep.

When I woke, he was still sitting there. He hadn't slept. I asked him to say something. He had such a look of hate in his eyes, "I thought this would be a new beginning for the two of us." He stood up left the room. I realized he wasn't taking me back to the orphanage. I dreaded what he might do. He didn't speak to me until evening. He came to fetch me for dinner. He told me that from then on, considering the situation, that I would have to be known as his wife. That it was, the only way, people wouldn't talk about my baby being a bastard and my being a whore.

I cried as he explained his decision. He said that he would take care of me and my child as long as I kept that promise. I asked him what about all the things he said we would do. He only looked at me and said, 'You've messed that up good and proper." I was stunned, "He blamed you!"

"Of course."

"You were a child, taken advantage of."

"He didn't see it that way. I think that was the last straw for Thomas. He changed, like his last bubble had burst. He did talk to me tho. He always talked to me. I suppose he needed someone to confide in. He once told me I was his family now, regardless. He grew less moody as my pregnancy progressed. We bought everything for the baby. I think he was excited a couple of times.

The day I went into labor only Thomas was around and he delivered the twins. I was as shocked as he was. Two tiny babies with flaming red hair. He made the comment that they looked just like their father. I thought that remark somewhat strange. They didn't look like me. Even under the circumstances I couldn't help but love them, they were so tiny and helpless. I know Thomas had hoped they would favor me, at least have dark hair. They would be easier to pass off as his.

The first year taking care of them was very tiring. The most Ida would do was the laundry, which helped, but not knowing much about babies it was quite hectic.

"Where was Thomas?"

"He was always away on business. Even when he was around, he only told me that, that was what motherhood was about. I was a good mother once I got the hang of it. They grew up healthy and strong.

"I agree." She frowned at my tone. "Do they give you trouble in

school?" I shook my head. "Just the opposite. They are extremely bright and answer my questions. I don't know they are very– quiet."

"You mean strange." I felt relieved. "Yes."

"I know. I thought they would grow out of it they were such happy babies. When they were able to walk and get around was when they turned sullen and introverted. I taught them to read and write at an early age and they enjoyed their books. They never wanted to play. It exasperated me. I tried to play games with them even something as simple as throwing a ball.   They would pick it up and look at it as if it were the strangest thing they'd ever seen. Then they would throw it with little enthusiasm. I worried they weren't getting enough exercise so I made them walk. When I found them sitting on the grass staring off, I forced them to follow me. At first they balked until I threatened to take away their books. So we walked, everyday, for an hour. The rest of the time they spent reading or staring.

I wanted to take them to the doctor, Thomas said they'd grow out of it, they haven't."

"Not that I can tell."

"I wish I could've done better by them. By the time they were eight was when Thomas actually took an interest in them. When school let out, he would take them with him on his business trips. I was happy they were at least getting out and seeing something of the world."

"Didn't you go?"

"No. Thomas said it was business and he knew I would be bored. He said it was best if I stayed here and looked after things."

"Didn't you have any friends, in town?"

"I tried but Thomas had already taken care of that."

"How so."

"Like I said he couldn't pass the twins off as his own, so he set about destroying my reputation. He couldn't even be kind about it. He told people that I had cheated on him and got pregnant. Some felt sorry for him, he built this town and they were grateful for it. Now he was strapped with a tramp for a wife and how noble he was taking her children on as his burden.

I heard the whispers and some weren't so quiet about it. I asked

Thomas why he did it. He only shrugged, "How else can I explain you?" You know, somehow, in the back of my mind I had the feeling that he wasn't quite right, I had no idea how vindictive he could be. So, I would go into town as little as possible and avoid the people I did meet.

"Would you have been able to explain?'

"Who would listen? These are his people, not mine. I had thought often about his threats of kicking me out without a penny, so I thought of a way to get some money of my own. He was always generous taking care of me and the boys, whatever I wanted he gave me ample money to buy it with. So I began skimming a little here and there and saving it up. Even if it took a couple of years, I would at least have a nest egg for us until I could find a job. That was my plan, but even the best laid plans, backfire."

She sat back and grew quiet. "I didn't mean to tire out. I haven't talked this much in years."

"I understand."

"I'm hungry."

"I can go downstairs and fix something."

"No need, I have a kitchen in the next room."

"Really!" She pointed the way and followed me. I was looking for the canned peaches she wanted. She put on the kettle. "This is amazing. I wondered how you managed by yourself. I thought someone, maybe, came by and helped you."

"I made Thomas do this. You won't believe it but this and my bathroom are the only rooms with electricity. "

"I do not understand why he chooses to live in such a manner."

"I don't know. You saw how long it took him to buy a car." I carried our tray back so she could stretch out on her chaise. We ate mostly in silence then I offered to wash the dishes, she said she would do it later. I could see in her eyes she was getting tired. "I thought if I ate I'd feel better but it only made me sleepy."

I told her I would come back in the morning. "Of course, we have plenty of time." She was drifting off as she spoke. I carried the tray back to the kitchen and washed them for her. She was sleeping *soundly when I returned. I covered her with a throw and left. I don't know why, but when I got downstairs to the door I felt a chill. I decided to go out the back way and around.*

December 19, 1919

This morning I went to her room and tapped lightly. "C'mon in." She was in her usual position. "Did you sleep well, Daniel?"

"No. And it's all your fault." I jested. She laughed. "Thank you for the blanket. I feel better, today. Do you have any questions you'd like to ask?"

"Are you kidding, a million, and yet I can't decide which to ask."

"Well, I thought about it, how about I give you some history on the town."

"Please do."

"I remember when I first arrived. We were met at the train depot by a little rat faced man named Kranston."

"Oh yes, I remember my encounter with him and his wife. Terrible."

"Don't feel too sorry for them. Anyway, there was quite a lot of construction going on since Thomas moved in. People were moving further away from the tracks, which was, the center of town, for the longest time. You remember the condition of the depot when you arrived?"

"Yes, they ran the hotel, as well."

"Humph. A rat's nest is more like it. I imagine you were the only one in the lobby that day?"

"Yes, I believe I was."

"Probably the only customer they'd had in months. Anybody that knows this town doesn't stay there. It's either with friends or family. Now they have a new hotel. That place is merely a rest stop between trains. When Thomas first arrived, they saw what he was doing and decided to give him a sad story of how if they had the means they could fix the place up and improve business. He had no idea that they were both drunks. He made a contract and loaned them the money. Of course that went for liquor and no improvements were made.

That infuriated Thomas and when he called the loan in, they panicked. He said they would have to vacate the premises and he would build a new depot. They cried and begged him not to put them out on the streets. He told them they had a week to come up with the money. So the week goes by and no money, so they gave him the only thing they had worth anything. Lettie."

"Their daughter?"

"Have you ever seen her?" I was embarrassed. "Don't worry Daniel."

"Well, now that you mention it, I haven't."

"Yes, she merely runs the place and keeps the books. Thomas wouldn't let her, work the floor. He actually felt bad for her that her parents would do something like that. As far as they know, she does work the floor, that's how he punishes them, he even goes there once in awhile to remind them what their daughter does for a living."

"That explains a lot. Why, don't they leave."

"No money. The place has been for sale for years, no one wants it. What little money they do make they drink up."

"Pitiful."

"Yes. That's how Thomas works. He finds your weak spot and pounces. You would know Lettie if you get a chance. Little Francis and Toby look just like her."

"NO! Those are her children. Where is the father?"

" He works the barges."

"He doesn't mind that his wife runs a whorehouse."

"Why, should he? They have grand plans of saving up plenty of money and leaving this place. They want their children to go to college."

"What about little Freddie?"

"They take care of him as well. He is the child of the father's sister. She died in childbirth and he was sent to live with them."

"How sad. So they don't see what goes on?"

"Oh no. They live away from the house."

"What about Ida and Peeler. What is their story?"

"I really don't know. It never came up. They were here when I arrived. They are fiercely loyal to Thomas. They tolerate me."

"Do they know you are his sister."

"Not, that I, know of. I'm sure he told them the same story he told people in town about me." I was quiet, absorbing everything I had heard. Thinking of Kranston brought forth a name I was curious about."

"What can you tell me about a Mr. Collins?" Her eyes widened. *"Where did you hear about him?"*

"When, I first arrived it was mentioned, I hope you last longer than Mr. Collins."

"Oh. I believe I'm going to need a brandy for that one." I hurried to grant her request. When settled I watched her sip her brandy. *"That's fine. Yes, poor Mr. Collins and his one moment of chivalry."* I watched her eyes as she remembered. She seemed amused." Is it that funny what happened?" She grew serious. *"Not at all. I think that, that was the only time I'd ever seen Thomas actually afraid."*

"Really. Don't keep me in suspense."

"Mr. Henry Collins was the schoolteacher in town when Thomas arrived here. After Lettie's was built Thomas noticed how frequently Collins visited. I only saw him one time he was much older than Thomas but he had a youthfulness about him. They became fast friends. I guess Thomas liked having someone for companionship. Although, he talked to me about everything, I wasn't approving of all his debauchery. They were a perfect pair, so Thomas thought. Thomas would go down to New Orleans to recruit new girls, when he came back with a trio one time Collins recognized one of the girls. She had come from a very fine family he used to be associated with and he recognized her right off. He told Thomas that she should go back to her family and not get dragged down any further. That made Thomas furious. He doesn't like it when people try to be phony.

"Yes, I remember him getting mad when I said I didn't think it proper considering my station."

"Exactly. If it is good enough for him, it is good enough for all. Collins separating this particular girl from the rest just because she came from a good family, unlike the others. Just because Collins didn't know them, who was he to judge. So they argued and Collins was

quite adamant about taking her back. Thomas said that once he had paid for something it was up to him what happened after. Collins even offered to buy her back Thomas only laughed because he knew he couldn't afford it on his salary.

I asked Thomas how the girl got in this situation. He said she'd got in trouble back home and went to New Orleans to save her family scandal. She had her baby but it died she went to work at a house down there to support herself. Collins booked passage on one of the boats going back, he told Thomas that no matter, he was going to make sure the girl went home. Then Thomas changed tactics and agreed with him and decided to go along.

When Thomas returned he was unusually quiet. I asked about Collins and the girl. He looked at me strangely and said that they were both dead. I was surprised, I urged him to tell me what had happened. He said that they had almost reached port when Collins and the girl began arguing. He said he was tired of listening and went to his cabin. When he came out a little later, they were both gone. He had to think fast, because a crew member noticed they were gone and called the police. They searched the boat they were nowhere to be found. They sent out boats and divers only Collins body was found. He said that he told the police what had occurred and the matter was settled as accidental drowning.

"What was he afraid of?"

"Well, I was reading the newspapers which carried an account of the accident. There was a particular detective involved in the case who didn't buy the theory of an accident. For one thing according to the coroner's report Collins didn't have any water in his lungs. There were bruises around his neck. They concluded that he was murdered and dumped in the water. Collins was a big man and the crew which had seen the girl said there was no way a tiny thing like her could have done something like that.

"Oh, my! Did they ever find the girl?"

" She was found on the bank two weeks later. She had been cut numerous times and her face was almost gone. Her family's retainer identified her because she had a prominent birthmark on her outer

thigh. They took her home and buried her. Thomas made arrange-
ments for Collins. The detective asked Thomas the same questions on
several different occasions, Thomas never wavered in his answers.

"So he thought they had him?"

"Yes. They had very little to go on. Nobody knew much else and
Thomas was sticking to his story. He told them that maybe the per-
son who called them did it. They really couldn't point the finger at
anyone. Eventually it died down. I think that was the closest he ever
came to being caught."

"The closest?

"Oh yes, Daniel. The man you are trying to out maneuver so he
won't bother you is a cold, blooded killer."

I was thoughtful. "How many do you think he's killed?" She shook
her head and a tear formed in the corner of her eye. "Too many."
She dabbed her eyes and sniffed. She emptied her glass and asked for
another. "I want you to be fully aware of what you are dealing with,
Daniel. I told you I would help you but you have to know your enemy
before you fight him. If you have to go through with this at all."

"Of course I have to. I don't like people lording over me, anymore,
than he does."

"Look at your face, Daniel." I went to the mirror. She slowly
walked up behind me. "Have you forgotten, already?" I looked at the
faint scars on my face. "No. I haven't forgotten." She put

her hand up to her veil. "That is what he did to you, because
he suspected, and rightly so, that you were going thru his things." I
nodded. "He labeled you a traitor. He labeled me as well for trying to
leave. I am his sister and this is what he did to me." She brought the
veil down. My eyes bulged. "Oh no! Oh NO!!!" I covered my eyes and
turned away from what that poor girl suffered.

I am crying now thinking of the image that stood by me in the
mirror. She had no face. Her cheeks had been slitted and now thick
wide scars remained. Her nose had been split on both sides making
the nostril flat. It looked as if his wanted to cut out her eyes in his
fury but stopped himself. So instead he sliced off her chin and cut
that horrible 't' in her forehead. She replaced her veil and grabbed

my shoulders. *"I'm sorry, Daniel. I know it's a shock. I only want you to know that your life will be at stake if you go thru with this."* I couldn't stop crying, I wasn't crying for me, here she was consoling me when she was the one to be consoled.

I, held her in my arms and stroked her back. I know she was crying as well and I didn't want her to. I pulled myself together and wiped my face. She kept patting my shoulder. *"Please, forgive me."* I begged. *"I know, Daniel, I know. What do you think I did when the bandages came off?"* I looked into those beautiful tormented eyes and I embraced her again. *"He has to pay, Emily. This seals it. It's not just about me getting away. He has to pay."*

I helped her back to her chaise and filled up the brandy glasses. *"Will you tell me why he did this to you?"*

"I don't know if I can. It's very painful to think about."

"I won't pressure you." I drained the brandy glass. *"I think I need a nap, Daniel. This has been, very unnerving."*

"I understand, Emily. I'll come back tomorrow."

"No. I need some time. I'll signal when I want you to come back." Her voice was weary. I wished I could do something for her. Her eyes were sad and worried. I think she regretted telling me anything. She was confused, she wanted revenge on her brother but at what cost? *"I'll open the balcony door when the time comes."*

"I'll watch for it." I knelt beside her and kissed her hand. *"You're a brave woman, Emily."*

"I don't feel brave." I told her goodbye and came home.

CHAPTER 6

BIZZLE HAD NODDED OFF knowing what Emily endured made him heart sick. He dreamed of their time together and the night she kissed him. He touched his fingers to his lips remembering the need and wanting that kiss generated. They had seen each other every night, going to plays and such. After a couple of days she had relaxed and acted like a school girl. Laughing at his jokes and the night they went for a canoe ride, she teased him by splashing water at him.

Things got out of hand and they tipped into the lake. She held onto him as he pulled her to shore. It was a warm night and they lay back on the grass looking at the stars. She told him of her time growing up at the orphanage and being best friends with Patty. She tried to make it sound happy but he could hear the loneliness in her voice. He asked her where she met her husband and she was quiet. "I don't want to talk about that, if you don't mind." She was regressing into her shell. Bizzle told her that he would never mention it again.

They lay there for a while and suddenly, Emily stood up and began pulling her dress off. "What are you doing!" Bizzle looked around for anyone that might be around. "I want to swim." In her chemise and bloomers she jogged to the edge and dove in. He watched her for awhile, she was beautiful in the moonlight. She paddled around for, awhile. She stopped and called for him to join her. He hesitated. She moved closer revealing her exquisite figure as the thin material plastered to her body. He peeled down to his shorts and dove in beside her.

They splashed around and she dove on top of him to push him under. He thought he'd tease her by staying under until he heard her calling for him, frantically. He jumped up from behind and grabbed her. She slapped at him and cried that he was mean. She hugged him in relief and he held her. She relaxed against his body and looked up. He wanted her but he wasn't going to make her do anything she didn't want to. Then she kissed him. She pulled back and looked at him then kissed him again wrapping her arms around his shoulders.

Chief Banes shook Caleb's shoulder. "Wake up, sleeping beauty." Bizzle blinked and rubbed his head. "Mom thought, you were in the bed." Banes noticed the empty scotch bottle sitting by the cold cup of coffee. Bizzle yawned, "What time is it?" "Seven." Bizzle rubbed his neck and absently looked about the room. He wanted a drink, badly.

"Make any progress with that journal?" Bizzle shook his head. "Only that Emily suffered at the hands of that monster brother of hers."

"Doesn't look as if you have very much left."

"I'm almost done. You're up early."

"Actually I just returned. I went to see Mr. Will or Mr. Arbaugh, whichever you prefer."

"What did he have to say?"

"He wouldn't talk. He looks pretty rough."

"Good. I hope he rots in that place this time."

"He will. We've brought other charges against him."

"Such as?"

"Lettie's, evidently, he supplied the girls."

"Lettie only kept the books."

"That's right."

"Trafficking minors across state lines for lewd acts, is a crime. We have numerous accounts and plenty of the girls have given statements."

"You've been busy since I saw you last."

"It wasn't difficult. Lettie approached me and confessed everything. She hoped it would help keep Thomas Will in prison.

"Why would she do something like that? From what I read she and her husband were happy with their little enterprise."

"She didn't say, but it doesn't matter, now."

"That must've riled him when you told him."

"No. Not a bit. He only sat there and smiled. I tried everything, couldn't get a rise out of him." Bizzle shook his head. "It's incredible." Banes continued, " I've never come across a psychopath." He let out a yawn. "Let's get some coffee, mom has it ready." Bizzle sipped his coffee as he told Banes what he'd read so far. "I'm sorry she had to go thru all that."

"I wish she'd confided in me. I would've done anything to have kept her from going back." In the hall the telephone rang, Mrs. Banes answered and motioned to Elliot the call was for him. Banes spoke quietly and hung up the receiver. He walked back to the kitchen, "They're releasing the bodies today. Coroner is coming by with the report. The funeral will be at three." Bizzle let out a breath. "Yeah." There was a knock at the front door. Banes made a face, "Busy mornin'"

When he returned, Mr. Calloway followed him. Bizzle stood up. "Mr. Bizzle." Calloway extended his hand. "Good morning." "Mr. Bizzle, in carrying out Emily Will's wishes I have this package for you." Bizzle hesitated before taking the box. "Also, if you would accompany me to my office, I have some documents that need to be signed and notarized in order to implement the release of the estate. "Very well. Let me get my coat.""Don't you want to open the box?" Banes, asked. Bizzle looked at the box then at Banes, "Not just yet."

Bizzle sat in shock in Mr. Calloway's office. It was slowly sinking in that he was now in charge of over twenty million dollars. "Good night! It will be a full time job taking care of all this."

"I'm sure you can handle it. Emily Will said she trusted you like no other." Bizzle shook his head, "I'm speechless." Calloway chuckled. "I understand. Here is my card if I can ever be of service." Bizzle thanked him and left. He wanted a drink.

When he arrived at the Chief's, Banes was sitting at the kitchen table. He was reading the journal. "Find anything new?" " Just passing time." Mrs. Banes offered breakfast. Bizzle declined asking for coffee instead. She poured him a cup and excused herself. "Here's the coroner's report."Bizzle took off his wet coat and hung it over the chair. "Will this rain ever end?" He mumbled. "What does it say?"

"Well, the blood on the door was Peaster's. Some blood from one of the twins, was on the knife handle. I figure, whichever one was doing the stabbing their hand slipped and they were cut." "So one of them did kill Peaster." "Yes. As far as the twins go, someone brained them with a sharp instrument. Around a three, inch, gash in each of their heads. Take a guess on what could've caused that." Bizzle sipped his coffee. "An axe?" "That's what I think."

"So, the fire was started after?"

"Possibly. Trying to cover it up. Evidently, Peaster managed to crawl away during the assault. That leaves us with figuring out who killed the twins."

"And Emily?"

"I don't think the attacker knew she was in the house. Peaster was under the impression she'd been sent to a sanitarium, until he ventured upstairs."

"Do you think the twins acted on their own?"

"I doubt it. Thomas Will probably had them so brain washed they would do anything he said." Bizzle shuddered visibly. "What is it?" Banes asked. "I just had a horrible thought. What, would've happened to Emily had they not been, interrupted?"

"I don't even want to think about it." Banes shuddered himself. "Say. What was in that box Mr. Calloway dropped off?" "I'll get it." He brought the package to the kitchen table and unwrapped it. A very ornate lid met Bizzle's eyes. He carefully lifted the lid. Banes caught Bizzle as he collapsed and sat him in a chair. Banes peered inside the box and brought out a photograph. "Emily Will. She was beautiful." Bizzle wiped his eyes and reached for the photograph. "This was taken at the amusement park the day before she left." Banes retrieved a small teddy bear from the box. "And this?" "I won that for her." Bizzle clutched the bear to his chest. Banes pulled out a last item. He handed Bizzle an envelope. His hands shook as he pried the letter away from the envelope.

My love,

Please, do not think ill of me for what I have done.

Remember always, that I love you. Please, remember me, sometimes.

Yours truly,

Emily

"Emily." Bizzle whispered. "How could she think I would not remember her?" Banes stepped out of the kitchen to let Bizzle collect himself. Mrs. Banes approached Elliot in the hall. He told his mother what had happened. "That poor boy." She stood beside Bizzle and put her arm around his shoulder, hugging him. "I'm so sorry, Caleb." Bizzle sniffed. "Thank you, Mrs. Banes." He gripped her hands and took a deep breath. "Things have been happening awfully fast for you." Bizzle nodded. "Yes, ma'am."

She stood beside him, "Listen. You need to eat something. You didn't have breakfast." Bizzle tried to protest, she waved him off. "Nonsense. You'll make yourself sick. Now go wash up and I'll make you some lunch." Bizzle gathered his things and went to his room. Banes stepped into the doorway. "You going to be all right?" Bizzle stared at him. "Did you ever love a woman?"

"Oh yes. Back in college."

"What happened?"

"She married someone else."

"That's too bad." Banes looked towards the bedroom window. "Yeah." He rubbed the back of his neck. 'You better do what mom says. She'll come looking for you." Bizzle tried to smile and headed towards the bathroom.

Even tho, Mrs. Banes, was a good cook, he couldn't taste any of the food he ate. He only did it to make her happy. She smiled at him as she took his empty plate away. Bizzle liked her immensely. It had been so long since he'd had a mother fussing over him. He managed to smile back at the sweet lady. Banes looked at his watch. "It's getting late, if you want to go to the cemetery." Bizzle nodded, "Right."

As Banes drove Bizzle thought of his and Emily's last days together. He met her in the hotel restaurant, she was beaming at him when he greeted her. Bizzle decided they would go to the amusement park. He remembered how her eye's lit up at the thought. They rode the trolley to the park. It wasn't very busy that time of year, which suited them both. She must have ridden the roller coaster five times. Bizzle didn't care for it but he delighted at her squeals and laughter and clutching at his arm.

Next was the carousel, then the ferris wheel. She had to try the cotton candy and the ice cream. They went on to the shooting gallery and the ring toss. He won a bear for her knocking down the milk bottles. She went on about how it had such a sweet face

They sat on a bench and watched the sun set. "What a glorious day, Caleb."

"I'm glad you enjoyed it." To his surprise she leaned over and kissed him. Her expression   touched him deeply. He took her hand and kissed the palm. "I love you, Emily." She caressed his cheek. "I love you, Caleb." He let out a sigh. "Show me where you live."

They arrived at his apartment. She tossed her things in a chair and walked around looking about. He brought her a glass of lemonade and she sat beside him on the sofa. "I'm so happy I met you, Caleb, I don't want it to end." He looked at her seriously. "It doesn't have to."

"What do you mean?"

"Stay with me, Emily. Stay with me forever." She abruptly stood. "I can't. I have to go back. At least for my children's sake."

"We'll go and get them. All that is yours, I want, here, with me." She wiped a tear away.

"Marry me, Emily." She began crying. "You don't understand, I can't." He held her in his arms. "Your husband. He can't stop you."

"You have no idea what you're saying." She sniffed back her tears and tried to smile. "Please, let's not talk anymore." Then she kissed him. Bizzle ached remembering the passion they shared.

He woke up the next morning and rolled over to kiss her awake. She was gone. He searched the apartment and was getting dressed to go look for her. She came in with a sack. "Good morning, Caleb." He dropped his shoes and rushed over grabbing her arms. "I'd thought you'd gone." He kissed her fiercely on the lips. "Well." She gasped. "I only went down the street to get some things for breakfast. Your cupboards leave a lot to be desired." Bizzle gazed at her face as if he were trying to burn her image into his brain.

"I wish you would've woken me." She broke from his grasp and headed to the kitchen.

"Don't be silly. You were sleeping so well, I didn't want to bother you." He stood in the doorway watching her dance about preparing the coffee. He ached for her beauty. She smiled at him. "The coffee will be ready soon. What would you like for breakfast, eggs or pancakes?" He walked over to her and took her in his arms. "I love you, Emily. In fact I am in love with you."

She smiled and kissed him tenderly. "I'm in love with you, Caleb. You are the dearest man I could ever imagine." He kissed her deeply. "Don't you know, Emily, I can't get enough of you? I can't get close enough. Please, stay with me. Like I told you before, we'll bring your boys here, we'll be together." She pulled away from him. "I have thought about it. Just let me go back and take care of some things and I will let you know. Do not, please, do not come for me until you hear from me.

He wanted to argue but she kissed him. "Promise me, Caleb, please." She was so lovely looking at him with her pleading eyes. How could he refuse her. "Alright, Emily. You think you know best how to handle this. I'll wait to hear from you." She was relieved. "Thank you. Now what do you want for breakfast?" Bizzle smiled at her, walked over to the stove and turned off the gas. She giggled when he turned to her. Then she squealed as he chased her to the bedroom.

Later that evening, he dropped her at her hotel so she could change her clothes. They were going out to dinner. He told her he had to go to his office and take care of a few things. An hour later he arrived and went to the lobby. She said she'd be waiting for him only he didn't see her. He asked the clerk if he knew anything. Bizzle was devastated when he told him she had checked out.

"Where did she go?" he demanded. "I do not know, sir. The lady merely asked for a cab to the train station, paid her bill and left."

Bizzle ran to his car and sped to the station. He searched everywhere. He found a porter and asked about the last train. "It pulled out about ten minutes ago, sir, they'll be another one in about twenty minutes." Caleb stood motionless, the porter shrugged and went about his business. Caleb stumbled over to a bench and collapsed. His first thought was to go after her but he remembered his promise. Maybe it will work out, he thought. He thought he would hear from her soon. He didn't doubt it. He went back to his apartment and poured out a scotch.

He collapsed on the bed. He could still smell her perfume and their lovemaking. *'I should go after her. Promise be damned.'* Her pleading eyes kept appearing to him. What was she so worried about. Bizzle thought. She was worried about me. She knew he would try something. He would never let her go. Bizzle put his hand over his eyes.

When they reached the cemetery, tarp, covered piles of dirt guarding four graves, greeted them. Banes parked close by. Ted met them and shook hands with them. "Didn't think you'd be here, Ted?" Banes spoke. "Looks like we're the only mourners, so to say, thought I'd come for moral support." He looked at Caleb. "Hope you don't mind?"

"Not at all. I appreciate it." Bizzle watched as they brought out the caskets. Banes whispered that the first two were Reginal and Phillip's. They were lowered into the ground. Emily's casket was next. His heart sank with the casket. Flashes of Emily alive presented themselves to Caleb. He wiped his eyes thinking of her at the park, splashing in the water, laying in his bed all shattered with the image of her burnt body, the sound of her gasp.

"Ashes to ashes, dust to dust." The pastor's words pulled Bizzle back to the present. Everyone said, 'Amen.' Men began shoveling the dirt. Banes clapped his hand on Bizzle's shoulder. "Are you ready?" Bizzle nodded but didn't move. Banes and Ted looked at one another and nodded, they walked away so he could have a moment alone. They hadn't begun filling in Emily's grave yet and he walked over to the edge and stared at the brown box the love of his life was now resting in. "Goodbye, Emily." He whispered, then turned and walked away.

Sitting in a booth at the café, the waiter served their coffee. Neither said a word. Bizzle gazed at the cloudy sky. At least it had stopped raining long enough for the burial. Banes was deep in thought when Bizzle spoke. "I should get back and finish that journal." "Finish your coffee and I'll take you home."

"I dread what it will say next."

"I don't know. It might help you understand why she left."

"It's awful, Elliot. Every time I think of her, how alive and beautiful she was. The way that I saw her yesterday always barges in and takes over."

"You've had a lot to deal with. C'mon, finish up."

Bizzle decided to read the rest in his room. Banes told him he had some things to take care of, he'd be back soon.

CHAPTER 7

December 26, 1919

It has been an entire week since I last saw Emily. Everyday, several times a day, I would go out to see if her door was open. I began to worry after the second day but I will have to give her time.

December 27, 1919

It was a close call today. I barely made it back to my cottage. I woke early and dressed. I was having my coffee when I decided to check her door. I walked out a few yards and it was open. I threw the cup down and ran to the house. I was going to knock only her bedroom door was open. "It's all right, Daniel, come in." I greeted her, she seemed in better spirits. "I'm sorry it took so long, Daniel, I haven't felt well." I nodded, "I understand, Emily. We didn't have to talk about the past, I would've liked to have spent time with you no matter what we talked about."

Her eyes narrowed. "The past is all I have." I felt like picking her up and taking her away from there, to hell with everyone and what may happen. Just to see her somewhere other than here. She had a box sitting by her. "I had to come to terms with what I'm going to tell you about why Thomas hurt me." I went to her. "Emily, if it is going to distress you, I would rather you didn't."

"No. You need to know, I have to tell someone." I sat down after I poured out the brandy. Strangely, she didn't drink it. She opened the box with trembling hands and took out a photo in a plain picture frame. She handed it to me. The woman in the picture was too beautiful for words. I couldn't take my eyes off of it. The curve of the brow the perfect lips and the eyes. My fingers tightened when I looked at the eyes. I looked at Emily, she nodded to me. My heart sank.

"That was taken a few years ago." I couldn't speak. What kind of demon could do what he did to her. I felt the tears well up, I wiped them away quickly. "I don't know what to say, except that I am sorry."

"You don't have to be sorry, he's the one who should be sorry." I looked at the picture one last time and handed it over. "As I mentioned, I had decided that I would save myself some money and that way I could take the boys and leave. I contacted my friend Patty in Cathage and told her, that I would be coming for a visit. She was happy to hear from me and I took the train down to see her. My plan was to try and find a job. I became very depressed after a week of looking. Since I had no special skills or schooling nobody would hire me. Even some of the places that didn't require experience didn't think I would do. I tried to find work just scrubbing floors, I did that often enough at the orphanage only they had all the help they needed.

I was sick at heart, even with the money I had what would I do when it ran out. I was sitting in the lobby of my hotel talking to Patty who was trying to cheer me up. She even tried to get me a job where she worked, only, they weren't hiring at the time. She said to give it some time that something would turn up. I was downhearted that my grand plan was backfiring. I thought that I should go back home and forget about it, then Patty said I should consider using the money I saved and go back to school. I brightened at that thought. Thomas wouldn't care, he thinks education is most important."

"Yet, he wouldn't send you to college."

"Well, not at the time but since the boys were older and didn't

require constant attention I would have the day to go to school myself.
He only said things had changed because of the children he didn't say
I could never go to school. So I talked it over with her and I decided
that was what I would do. It wouldn't take that long, another couple
of years to go through secretary school then I could get a job and get
away.

I was feeling better about the situation and she got up to go buy
something, gum I think, while she was away, a man approached me.
He was very handsome and very forward. I didn't know what to make
of it. My first thought was that Thomas was having me followed. I
tried, to act casual about the whole thing, I didn't want to cause a
scene. I hoped if he was following me he would see that I wasn't a
nervous kitten. I wasn't going to run screaming into the night. He
finally left and I thought that was the end of it.

He showed up that night in the restaurant. I thought he was the
strangest detective I'd ever know about. I thought they lurked around
this one was bold. Then, I thought, he was sent to get me in a com-
promising situation and tell Thomas what happened. I decided to ask
him what he did for a living and he told me he was in fact a detective.
He went on talking as if nothing were wrong asking if I wanted to
go out to see a show or hear some music. I had enough by then and
went to my room.

He sent me flowers with a card that said he wasn't hired by anyone,
that he would follow me anywhere for nothing. I still didn't think I
could trust him and yet in his persistence he won me over. I realized
for the first time in my life that someone could actually like me, for
me. Not try to use me or hurt me. I don't know why but after spend-
ing a few days with him I felt as if I knew him all my life. I was so
comfortable with him so in love. He loved me to. I wanted to stay
with him forever, he even offered to help me come and get the boys
and live with him. He wanted to marry me.

It was so much like a dream. Then reality hit with a vengeance. I
had seriously considered taking him up on his offer but I received a
note at my hotel that put everything in perspective. He had dropped
me off and I was going to change my clothes so we could go to dinner.

He went to his office to take care of some business while I did so. The desk clerk stopped me. He had a nervous look on his face when he handed me the note. I almost collapsed when I read it. It said

Dear Emily,

I suggest you leave town if you are smart. I'll leave him alone if you will.

It was in Thomas' hand. I panicked and ran upstairs as fast as possible, threw my things together and hailed a cab.

"He knew the whole time?" I asked.

"Somehow. I never saw him when I was out but how does anyone know. Maybe, he had someone follow me. I don't know. I only knew, I had to get away from there. If anything happened to my love, I couldn't live with myself. I knew Thomas wouldn't hurt him if I did leave. I felt terrible having to do it that way but I was afraid. When I arrived home, he ranted and raved about my sneaking off behind his back. I told him I didn't know I had to ask permission every time I wanted to do something.

He threw things and broke up the furniture, that is why there are so few things in the house. He smashed all the pictures we had, photos and paintings. Ida had a devil of a time cleaning that mess up. "So he didn't hurt you then?"

"No. That would come later. I wrote to Caleb telling, him I was sorry I had to leave the way I did only he never answered me. I was hurt. I had doubted our time together. Was he only using me or did he really love me? I knew I loved him. I made myself believe he loved me. I thought he might be busy with his work and couldn't answer me. A few weeks later I had a bigger concern on my hands. I was pregnant. I was frantic. What would Thomas do if he found out? I knew, I had some time before I began to show. I wrote to Caleb telling him what was going on and that if he still wanted me I would be waiting for him.

Another month went by and I didn't hear from him. I called his apartment. There was no answer. I called his office and his secretary said he was out on business and she would tell him I called. I waited and waited. I never felt so alone in my life. I wrote to my friend Patty and told her what was going on.

She didn't answer my letter. Thomas had left again so I packed my bags and went to her. As soon as I arrived, I tried to reach Caleb but he was always away. I went to his office hoping to catch him there, only his secretary told me he was out. She acted nervous but was adamant that I should wait for Caleb to contact me. I left my address at the hotel and walked out.

I went to Patty's apartment, a lady answered the door. She said she'd been living there only a few weeks and that she didn't know what happened to Patty. I was frantic. I went to her place of work and they said they hadn't seen her in some time. One girl caught up with me and said she thought that Patty had met a man and had gotten married. Why wouldn't Patty tell me? I went to the hotel where I'd met Caleb and took a room.

It was getting closer for the baby to come. I went to his apartment, I knocked and knocked but there was no answer. I couldn't find anyone around so I went back to the hotel. I was distraught, I couldn't believe that I was missing him every time. I hung onto the words he spoke about, telling me that he loved me and that my children were welcome to live with him. That he wanted to marry me." She cried out painfully, 'That he loved me! If I could only see him!" She dabbed at her eyes and continued.

"My labor pains began and I took a taxi to the hospital. She was a beautiful little girl. I named her Colleen after my middle name. When it was time to fill out the birth certificate, I gave her Caleb's last name. The nurse taking the information wanted to know where my husband was I told her he was away on business. Somehow I don't think she believed me but she put the name down just the same.

"I knew I couldn't stay and I knew I couldn't take the baby back with me. I couldn't get in touch with Caleb. I didn't know what to do. Thomas would find me if I didn't go back and what money I had wouldn't get us very far away. I had to keep my baby safe until I could figure out a way to take care of her. I couldn't let Thomas get his hands on her. So I took her to the only place I could think of. The orphanage where I grew up.

I wouldn't leave her there for long. I would sell everything I had to get enough money to get her and get away. What a fool I was. They let me out of the hospital, after a week. I then took her to, Mrs. Tuttle's. I filled out all the papers and almost fainted when I had to hand her over to them. I wanted to die. My baby was in an orphanage and my son's were back home. I had no way of saving any of them. I cried the entire way home.

Caleb Bizzle lie back on the bed with his arm over his eyes. Tears streamed down the sides of his face. "I have a daughter." He rolled on his side and curled up. "I have a daughter." It was late when he pulled himself up. His head ached and he was sick to his stomach. He rifled thru his suitcase and found another bottle of Scotch. He gulped after swallowing half the contents. Letting out a belch the room began to spin.

He stumbled his way to the bathroom and splashed water on his face. He thought he would retch, he was able to stop it. He pulled his shirt off and splashed his face and chest. He ran his fingers thru his wet hair and looked disgustedly at his image in the mirror. "You have a daughter."

He wiped up his mess with his shirt and went back to his room. He lighted a cigar and brought the journal with him to the chair. It was misting and a cool breeze wafted in the open window. Feeling somewhat revived he picked up the book and began.

When I arrived home I was heart sick about leaving my baby I wanted her with me. I should have stayed but he would have tracked me down. I didn't know what else to do Daniel I didn't know what else to do." Her eyes pleaded for my understanding. I held her in my arms. "Please, Emily, please. You did what you thought was right. You were thinking of your child. I understand. Shhh." Her sobs lessened and soon she recovered.

" Thomas met me at the door. He was livid. 'How could you?' That was all he said. He dragged me upstairs and that is when he attacked me. I fought as best I could. At one point the knife was so bloody it slipped out of his grasp. I grabbed it and swiped at him, I know I

cut him once because he yelped. Blood was running into my eyes and I couldn't see and he pried the knife from my hands. With all my screaming no one would help me. I finally lost and blacked out.

Sometime later I woke up but I couldn't open my eyes. I was scared that I was blind. I was about to speak when I heard Thomas' voice thru my bandages. 'Just like her.' He was saying. He was sitting on the edge of the bed and holding my hand. "How could you do it? You didn't even know her and yet you're exactly like her. Just like her. I should kill you like I killed her but you're the only family I have. I think this will be better for both of us. The first time I saw you I thought it was my mother standing in that yard with those other girls. I thought that this was my second chance to take care of her. I wasn't a child anymore.

Of course you had to go and ruin it having those boys. I thought I would let it pass, give you a chance to be a good mother, and you were for awhile but that wasn't enough was it. You had to leave and just like her you got pregnant again. I know you were with that man. Why did you have to do it. Then you try to keep it a secret just like she did. I decided the only way I could save you from yourself was to take away the one thing that ruined both of you.

I'm not a child anymore and I'm not running this time. You'll have a reminder everyday of what happens to stupid girls that think if they have a man's child he will marry them and every one lives happily ever after. That's what she thought. All she managed was bringing two bastard's into the world.

I lived with her in that stinking attic until I was ten. That man she worked for a Mr. Richard Arbaugh, was an arrogant son of a bitch. He didn't pay her much and she worked like a dog. Early one morning I was awakened by a terrible sound. I crawled out of bed and walked to the bathroom where she was kneeling on the floor, retching. I'd never seen her so sick and it scared me. She saw me standing there and told me to go ready for school. I tried to help her up and she snapped at me. That was the first time she ever raised her voice to me. I did what she said.

I cried the whole way to school. Something was wrong and she wouldn't tell me and she told me, everything. I would help her with her work when I wasn't in school. She was so lovely. I noticed how men would look at her when we went to town to do the marketing. She never spoke about her own family saying there were too many bad memories. I loved her so much I was proud to be seen with her in town.

That night I was getting ready for bed when the door at the bottom of the stairs slammed shut. Foot steps banged all the way up until I saw her in the door way. My heart raced seeing the expression on her face. "YOU!" That was all she could say. She stomped into the bathroom and slammed the door. I went to her to ask what was wrong and she slapped me. She had never hit me but this hit rocked me back and I banged my head on the wall. She grabbed me by the arm taking me back to my bed. "Go to sleep, Thomas. We have a lot of things to do in the morning."

I hid myself, under the covers, peeking out, watching her pack all our things. When she had finished, she didn't even change her clothes, she only laid down on her bed and was quiet. I don't know when I fell asleep, I only know it was still dark out when she was waking me. I rubbed my eyes. "Get dressed, we're leaving." I saw she was already dressed and was putting her hair up. I got dressed as fast as I could and she picked up our one bag and led me downstairs.

The house was quiet. 'Where are we going, mama?' She hissed at me to be quiet. We made it out the front door and it wasn't until we were well out of sight of the house did she speak.

"I have another job, Thomas, a better job." I was trying to keep up with her she was walking so fast. 'Where, mama?" "Mrs. Blake. I'm not staying in that house another minute. You will have to help me, Thomas. You won't be able to go to school."

"That's okay." She stopped short and faced me. "And you won't be able to call me, mama, anymore, either." I was confused. "Why?"

'Because, the old lady won't take me if I have children so now you'll have to be my brother and call me Kathleen. Do you understand?"

"Why do I have to be your brother?"

"How else am I going to explain you? Now lets practice. Thomas—'

she looked at me with glaring eyes. I whispered, 'yes, Kathleen.' "Good. Don't forget it."

"When we reached Mrs. Blake's house, a stern looking man let us in. He led us into a big library where a heavy set old woman with a mean looking, face sat behind a huge desk.

She didn't say a word, she just raised her glasses and looked us up and down. "I thought you were alone, girl." Kathleen curtsied, "Yes, ma'am. I apologize, for not mentioning him. He's my brother. I know he will be a great help, Mrs. Blake." The old woman stared at her for a moment. "Where are your parents?"

"They've passed away. We are alone, ma'am." Mrs. Blake cleared her throat. "I see. I hope you don't think I'll pay an extra wage?

"Oh no, ma'am."

"He'll have to stay with you. I don't have accommodations for an extra."

'Yes, ma'am. We're use to sharing. Thank you." I never took my eyes off the old lady. She didn't look as if she completely believed Kathleen. "If he breaks anything, it comes out of your pay. Simmons, show them to their room and explain her duties." Simmons who'd been standing like a statue the whole time bowed and walked out of the room. We followed him. Up the stairs we went. Only this room was smaller than at our other house.

Simmons talked the whole time telling her what she would be doing. She sat our bag down and he told her that 'madam' liked her dinner served promptly at noon then he turned and left. I watched her change into her work clothes. She didn't say a word to me until she had finished then she told me to put our things away and come find her in the kitchen. I didn't want to be there but what could I do. I joined her in the kitchen and she was looking thru all the cupboards. She told me to light the oven. I made a mistake and said 'yes, mama'.

She grabbed me by the arm and slapped me. "What do I have to do to get it thru your head, Thomas? You call me Kathleen, or else." I told her I was sorry. That was the last time I called her mama. Day after day we worked. The old lady was very demanding concerning her laundry and how the house was to be kept. She didn't have any* *complaints about Kathleen's cooking, tho.*

I could see Kathleen was getting very fat. I didn't see how she hardly ate and she worked constantly. Yet, she kept getting bigger and bigger. I had to help her carry the laundry down to the cellar where the boiling pots and scrub boards were. Eventually I was carrying them down by myself and taking them out to hang on the line. We didn't talk like we used to, she always looked at me with a kind of hate I had never seen before. One night when I was lying in bed watching her brush her hair, she began sobbing.

I went over to her. "Kathleen. What is happening? Why are you so sad?" She only shook her head. "You wouldn't understand, Thomas. Now go to bed I'm going to need your help tomorrow." I went to bed but I didn't sleep. The next day Mrs. Blake was demanding her tea. I carried the tray in and Kathleen began to pour. I stepped out of the room and waited. When she had stirred in the milk and sugar she turned to leave. "Wait.' the old woman barked. 'I want a word with you."

Kathleen was facing me, she looked scared. "Yes ma'am.' She went and stood in front of the old woman. "It looks as if you're putting on some weight?" Kathleen let her breath out. "I suppose, ma'am." Mrs. Blake inclined her head. "How do you explain it? Don't you have enough to do, or are you working that poor boy while you sit around eating my food?" Kathleen jumped, "No, ma'am."

"I think a few more chores will help take off the weight. Try scrubbing the front stoop and washing all the windows inside and out. That is all." She dismissed her, Kathleen looked more tired than ever. When we got back to the kitchen I told her I would wash the windows while she scrubbed the stoop. She handed me a pail and some rags and got her things together and headed outside.

That night she fell asleep with her clothes on. I tiptoed over and covered her. I tried to kiss her cheek but she slapped at me and rolled over. Even in her sleep she didn't want me touching her. Later that night I was jolted awake with her screaming. I ran to her, Her face was flushed and tear stained. She was panting hard. "Help me, Thomas, help me." She screamed and I ran for the door. I had to find a doctor. I ran straight into Simmons who was standing outside. He had towels and a tub of water. "Wait outside, boy." was all he said and he slammed the door in my face. I sat on the step crying, listening to her screams and calling for him. She was calling for Mr. Arbaugh.

She never asked for me she wanted him. I didn't understand why. She left his house and talked as if she hated him. A little while later I heard the crying. A baby crying. I stood up and listened at the door. A while later Simmons opened the door and looked at me. "Take care of your mother, Thomas." He bypassed me and went downstairs. I tiptoed into the room. It was quiet now. She looked up at me and smiled.

"Come here, Thomas, see your sister." I stepped up to the bed and saw you, Emily. You were beautiful and I loved you from that moment. "Are you alright, Kathleen?" Her smile faded. "It's alright, Thomas you can call me mama." No, I thought not anymore.

The next morning Simmons was knocking at the door he called out that Mrs. Blake wanted to see all of us. Kathleen looked frightened but I had a feeling we weren't welcome there anymore. I was right. We stood in front of the old woman while she sneered at us. "I don't like liars, Kathleen. You lied about him and you lied about that. Fat indeed. I knew you were with child the minute I laid eyes on you. You will leave this house immediately." We were dismissed.

I helped her upstairs and she told me to pack our bag. "Where are we going?" She wiped at the tears in her eyes and whispered. "Back." So back to Arbaugh's we headed. He actually answered the door when she rang the bell. "I knew you'd be back, my pretty." He winked at me. "Say, what do you have there?" He pulled back the blanket over your face. "Your daughter." He smiled at Kathleen. "So you say." He grinned. "You know it as well as I do. Just like he's your son." I was stunned. He was my father. I never knew who my father was, and the whole time I'd been living under the same roof with him.

"So he's my son. She's my daughter. I still won't marry you, Kathleen."

"Why!" She screamed. "You don't think I would ever marry below *my station. You're a servant for crying out loud. It just isn't done."*

"You snake, you said you loved me."

"I do, Kathleen. Even when you left me without a word and de-cide to come back expecting me to take you in. If I didn't love you I wouldn't have let you in the house." He sat down and looked up at her. "Now be a good girl and fix me something to eat. I haven't had anything decent since you left." She growled at him then you began fussing. She told me to get the kitchen ready and took you upstairs to feed you.

I never knew people could be so cruel, Emily. They spoke to one another as if I weren't there. She never told me a thing and now she had another baby by him and he still wouldn't marry her. For the first time I felt hatred for her for being so stupid. I knew what a bastard was and now she had two. She never tried to explain anything to me and of course Arbaugh didn't talk to me anyhow. I didn't really want to know her reasons or excuses. I had a strange feeling with me from then on and I couldn't shake it.

Things went back to the way they had always been except now I had the responsibility of taking care of you. I didn't go back to school and she only paid you attention when it came time to feed you, other-wise you were mine. One night I woke up to you crying and I knew you needed changing. It wouldn't be long before you would be hungry. It was late and I saw that Kathleen wasn't in bed.

She would at least stir if you were crying. I went downstairs to find her so she could feed you soon. The house was dark I went to the kitchen and the front room she was nowhere to be found. I couldn't imagine where she would be. Then I heard laughter. It was coming from Arbaugh's room. No, I thought not in his room. I crept down the hall by the dim light coming from his room. His door was partially open and I peeked my head round to see if she was in there.

All I saw was red. There she was completely naked with him. They were wrestling around and giggling. How could she? After what she had been thru, after what she had put, me thru. She was in that man's bed and she was happy. They didn't see me come in. I picked up the heavy irons from the fireplace and I struck Arbaugh on the head. He rolled off with a grunt. 'Thomas! What are you doing?" She screamed. "You whore!" I screamed back and hit her in the head. She collapsed beside him.

I went to the side of the bed and smashed the oil lamps on the table. I went to every room and smashed every lamp in them. I threw the irons down and went upstairs to get you. I packed our bag and brought you down. I made up some bottles with sugar water in them, you'd be getting hungry soon. I put you down in the hall and took the oil lamps from our room and slung the oil everywhere. I got you out the front door and amazingly enough you hadn't woke up.

I went back inside and I struck the matches. I was about to drop them when I heard her calling out to me. I almost blew them out until I heard her yell. "You've killed him. Richard, wake up!" That was all it took. I dropped the matches and the oil caught. I stood there and watched the trails brighten the house. I heard her scream when the flames went into their room. I turned around and stepped outside shutting the door.

I walked across the street with you and sat on the curb. You were beginning to fuss so I gave you a bottle and watched. I saw her at the window beating on the glass but the curtains were burning around her and she disappeared from view. You know the rest Emily, we were taken away. That despicable Judge Rains passing that sentence on me. No one would listen to my side. Now you know why I had to do what I did. Beauty is only skin deep, Emily. You'll have to accept that.

He got up and walked out of the room. I wanted to scream but I controlled myself. I don't know if he thought I was asleep or not but I wasn't going to give him the satisfaction of knowing I'd heard every word." She leaned back and was quiet. "I don't know what to say Emily. This entire time I've been here it's like a nightmare."

"I agree. My whole life has been a nightmare. My time with Caleb, was a brief moment of, something normal. That was the way life could be. Someone you love loving you. That was then. This is in fact the harsh reality."

"How did Mr. Will deal with the doctor?"

"Doctor?"

"Yes. To bandage you."

"There was no doctor. Thomas stitched me up and bandage my face. The same way he set my legs."

"When? I paused. "That morning when the door panes were broken?"

"Yes. You remember that? He had seen you waving up to me on occasion and that time he caught me waving back. He stormed about saying that I was stupid and that it would take more for me to learn my lesson. He threw me down and jumped on my legs until he heard them crack. All the time yelling that if I couldn't get about then I wouldn't be able to flirt with any man. When he calmed down, he set them and bandaged them.

It took me quite awhile to walk again. By this time he actually felt so guilty that he left me alone. No matter what I said or did he wouldn't come near me. He'd still talk to me but he gave up on trying to hurt me. I told him one more time and I would die and then who would he have. I guess he believed me and didn't want to take the chance. Of course they didn't heal properly but I manage."

Instantly she sat up. "Listen!" Her eyes were huge. "Does that sound like a carriage approaching?" I ran to the window. I saw Ida and Peeler's carriage about to turn into the drive. "Hurry! Go out the back." I ran to the door. "I'll see you, as soon as, I, can." She urged me to go. I ran down and headed for the kitchen. I could hear the hoof beats coming up the path. I ran to the other side of the house and peeked around to see their carriage disappear from view. I decided to run into the woods and disappear into the thick.

Since the trees were bare now, I had plenty of light to find my way. I kept looking back until I couldn't see the house anymore. I knew they couldn't see me. I kept walking until I found my path I'd taken so many times in the dark. It was strange seeing my surroundings in the daytime. I could now see the furrows and ditches, I'd stumbled over so many times. I kept walking and looking then I stopped. For some reason they didn't appear as natural formations, more like graves.

I stopped myself. I realized that Emily's terrible story was making my imagination get the better of me. I walked on shaking my head *telling myself to calm down. Still, I couldn't shake the eerie feeling I had. When I reached the edge of the clearing, I drew up short. Mr. Will was standing at my door waiting. I took a deep breath and went to meet him.*

"How are you Mr. Peaster? I didn't think I'd find you."

"Taking a walk, needed to stretch my legs. May I help you with something?"

"Thought I would treat you to supper." I cleared my throat. "That would be grand." I climbed in the seat beside him. He started the engine, "Then I thought we would go to Lettie's. They say you haven't been in awhile."

"I am saving my money to buy another horse." I looked at him as he chuckled. "Really! I hope you don't let this next one get away."

December 28, 1919

I woke up this morning in my own bed. I don't remember how I made it back home. My head felt like a ton of rocks were sitting on it. I forced myself to at least roll over. My whole body ached. It took me awhile to sit up. The room had a strange glow about it. I closed my eyes and sat there for the longest time. Eventually, I made an effort to stand. As soon as I did that I retched. I sank to the floor waiting for the nausea to subside.

I knew that I had went to Lettie's with Mr. Will and had one drink and that is all I remember. I pulled myself up by the bed. I needed to bathe, badly. I pulled my shirt off and happened to look down as I was unfastening my trousers, when I saw the blood. Panic took over as I hurried to see the damage. From the amount of blood I knew I was injured badly. When I got them off I went to the mirror to see. Everything was blood stained yet I felt no pain. I poured out a tub of water and washed. There was nothing. Where the hell did the blood come from.

I took my clothes to the sink and pumped the water. I was straining to remember what happened, to no avail. I scrubbed at my trousers but the water was to murky. As it drained a flash of a girls face appeared. Her eyes were bugged out and her mouth open as if she were gasping for air. That was all. I pumped more water and scrubbed harder. It took four times to get all the blood out but I could still see the outline of the stain. I threw them on the floor and crawled back in bed.

It was evening when I woke. I still felt groggy but not like this morning. I dressed and went up to the house. Ida was clearing the table when I walked in. The twins had been dismissed Mr. Will sat by himself. Ida brought me a plate and left the room. I pushed the plate away.

"You seem troubled, Mr. Peaster." I wanted to laugh but I didn't have the strength. "It's nothing."

"I think murder is something." My head flew up. "What are you talking about?"

"The poor girl, who's blood is on your trousers."

"No. I cut myself is all."

"You're a piss poor liar, Mr. Peaster."

"I don't remember anything about a girl."

"You never do." He smiled. I was feeling nauseated. "What?"

"I said you never do. This is the first time there has ever been blood." I squeezed my eyes shut as he continued. "Usually, you only strangle them."

"No! I refuse to believe any of this. It's a lie. I have never killed anyone in my life."

"Don't get upset."

"Don't get upset! You're accusing me of murder and you tell me— wait a minute. How do you know so much?"

"Who do you think takes care of things when you go off on one of your tangents. You should stop drinking, Mr. Peaster, you are quite a monster when you're drunk."

"You're insane!" He glared at me. "You forget yourself, Mr. Peaster." I ran my fingers thru my hair, nervously. "No, I didn't kill any of those girls. I don't even remember them."

"It costs a lot of money to replenish the inventory you dispose of so carelessly."

"Why?" I cried.

"Why what?" He asked, cooly.

"Why do you do this? Why did you bring me here? Why are you hell bent on making me miserable?"

"Am I? I told you a long time ago that I liked you. I still do. Now you're getting sloppy and I don't like sloppy. It's one thing killing a whore, it's quite another cleaning up the mess."

"You clean up and bury them?"

"No.' he chuckled. "I said I took care of things. Still, it costs money to keep everyone's mouth shut. You owe me quite a lot. I figure that if I pay you, half salary you will have to work here for another twenty years."

"So it's about keeping me here."

"If you like." He smiled. I felt like asking him if this is what he and Mr. Collins did together, then it hit me. He was waiting for me to slip and say something, anything that would prove I had been talking to Emily. That was all he would need and then he would feel justified to get rid of me as he pleased. I looked at him he was staring at me as tho he were trying to read my thoughts.

I regained my composure. I would play his game but on my terms. "Then stay, I shall." I stood up from the table. "Good evening, Mr. Will." His smirk faded. I turned and walked back to my cottage. Sitting here now I still can't comprehend the lengths he was willing to go. Still, the flash of that girls face and the blood on my trousers meant that something happened the question was, did I actually do it?

I have gone over my copy of his address book and have found the name Chauncey. No indication whether it was a first or last name. If this is the same man why, would he have the address of the man, who raped his sister. Another name on the list caught my eye. Harold Rains. Could it be the judge Emily mentioned? I have to go and find him. The next time Mr. Will leaves will be my chance. My only chance I'm afraid.

April 8, 1920

Mr. Will has never stayed at home for such a long time as this. Things have settled down. School is school and the boys will be going off to college next term. Francis is a beauty. For his age, Toby is as tall as the twins. Little Freddie is growing but I don't think he'll meet Toby's size. If I am here next term, it will be nice with the twins gone.

April 29, 1920

Francis was acting strange today. She wasn't her usual smiling self. I approached her at lunch and she nearly fell off the bench she was so nervous. "What is the matter, Francis?"

"Nothing, sir." Her hands shook as she packed her lunch away she hadn't eaten. "Anything wrong at home?" She shook her head. "Are you not feeling well?" She turned on me with tears in her eyes. "No! Mr. Peaster, I don't feel well, I can't talk to you about it." I told her, I understood, and let her be.

May 6, 1920

Francis hasn't attended class for a week now. All Toby would say is that she is ill.

May 9, 1920

My beautiful Francis has died. Toby said she had a fever and lost consciousness. She was dead by morning. He and Freddie are distraught as I am. The twins, of course, show no emotion as usual. I let school out for the rest of the day and let them go home with my condolences. Mr. Will was upset by the news. We both sent flowers to her house.

May 25, 1920

These last three weeks have been somber. Toby and little Freddie only sit at their desks, staring out the window. I thought of going to Lettie to see if there were something I could do. I thought better of it.

May 30, 1920

At last, Mr. Will said he was going. I said my goodbyes at dinner and came home. I have a bag packed and my money for the train ready.

June 1, 1920

I watched Ida and Peeler leave. Then waited for Mr. Will's car. Almost an hour later he turned out of the drive. I waited a while in case he turned back. When I felt it was safe I ran to the house. Emily was sitting on her chaise. I told her what my plan was. "Daniel!" She cried and held her arms out to me. I embraced her. "I'm going." She pulled back. "Now?"

"I have to. This may be my only chance." She looked down at the floor. I sat next to her. "What is it, Emily?" There were tears in her eyes. "I'm scared, Daniel." I took her hand. "Don't be. Everything, will be all right." I tried to sound convincing. "You don't want me to do this?'

She thought for a moment. "No. I want you to do this just not right at this moment. Do me a favor."

"Of course."

"Carry me downstairs." I was surprised. "What for?" Her eyes narrowed. "I want to make a phone call." I felt a little bewildered. "Don't worry, Daniel. I want to call our attorney." "I don't understand." She took a deep breath. "Because, if Thomas is going to prison, I want to know what my financial situation will be." I smiled at her. "Are you sure you can trust him?" "Why not? At this point it's all or nothing. I'd only feel better knowing." I picked her up and carried her down. She looked around the house. "My goodness, this place is bare, isn't it?"

She walked into the kitchen and with authority placed a call to William Calloway. When she hung up, she turned and smiled. "He'll be here shortly. Let's sit at the dining table and have a cup of tea." I put on the kettle and sat out the cups. She gazed at the room. "My! It's been a long time since I've been down here." I smiled at her. "Just think some day you can have one of those lift chairs put in then you can come and go as you please."

"We'll see." The kettle was steaming and I poured out our tea. "Feeling better?" She nodded. "Much. After, Mr. Calloway leaves you can go." She said. "I understand." We were on our second cup when a car pulled up. I met him at the door. "William Calloway." He greeted me. I showed him into the dining room. He took no notice of Emily's predicament he was all business. I sat by as he and Emily spoke together.

"All of Thomas Will's businesses and holdings are in your name."

Emily sat up. "Since when?" "Almost twenty years." She looked down, "He did this before he came for me."

"I don't understand?" Mr. Calloway said. "Never mind. You mean I've owned everything this entire time." "He didn't tell you." She shook her head. "No. What is it worth?" Mr. Calloway rifled some papers until he found what he wanted. "In the area of twenty million dollars." Emily covered her face with her hands. Mr. Calloway only looked at his papers. I rubbed Emily's shoulder. She dried her eyes and cleared her throat. "Mr. Calloway, I need to make out my last will and testament."

Mr. Calloway took down her instructions and said he would have the documents ready for her signature in a few days. When I returned from showing him the door, Emily had a strange look in her eyes. "You're a rich woman, Emily." "Yes. I suppose I am." I held her hand. "Don't mind me, Daniel. It's just the irony of it all." I understood how she felt. She gripped my hand. "Would you take me upstairs?" I, carried her up. "I'll, be back in a couple of days." She had tears in her eyes as she waved me goodbye.

June 3, 1920

I'm on the train home. I haven't felt so excited, I can't wait to tell Emily what happened.

I arrived at the Carthage depot around six thirty. I took a room at a nearby hotel. I purchased a map of the city and studied it. I located Chauncey's street and marked my route. I didn't have that much money so I would have to walk there.

The streets were buzzing with the evening crowds. I was nervous that I might run into Mr. Will. Nevertheless, I persevered in my quest. An hour later I found Caston street. I counted off the houses and stopped when I saw Mr. Will's car. It was parked in the driveway. My heart was beating fast. I took a couple of breaths to calm down. I wanted to sneak up and peer in the window. I was about to move when the front door opened.

From where I was standing I could hear a man speaking loudly. Mr. Will stepped out on the porch looking angry. He slammed the door and stomped to his car. Racing the motor, he backed out and sped down the street. I waited a moment by the hedge I had ducked behind. I felt it safe and stayed low making my way to the side of the house. Peering into the window I saw an old man, sitting in a wheelchair, it appeared he was still ranting.

So that was the monster who violated Emily. Look at him now. I could see the twins sitting on a battered sofa staring into space. Was this how they spent their time on all those breaks? All at once Reginal stood up and walked towards the window I was at. I crouched as close to the wall as possible. He raised the window. The odor, that leached out, made me want to gag. I took a chance and looked up. He had his back to me. I stayed where I was. Chauncey was blabbering on, I couldn't make out what he was saying.

I saw Reginal move away. Swallowing hard I rose up to see where he was, only I couldn't see either of them. I panicked when I moved further to see they weren't in the room at all. I sprinted back to my hedge. Gathering my courage I parted the branches. They were standing by the side of the house where I had been.

They didn't appear concerned, maybe they wanted a break from the odor. I thought of my predicament. What if some of the neighbors saw me creeping around. I had to get out of there. Finally, they turned and ambled toward the back yard. I waited until they were out of sight and dashed from my spot. I made it to the corner and rested. I was wet with sweat I wanted to go back to my hotel.

Exhausted when I reached my room, I collapsed on my bed. I could've sworn I saw Mr. Will drive by as I walked. I didn't stop to look back if it was. The next morning I dressed and placed a call to Judge Rains. I was connected to his secretary. I told her it was urgent and she gave me an appointment for ten thirty. While eating breakfast, I mapped out my course to the courthouse.

An hour later I was sitting in the outer office perusing a magazine when he strode in. He was an impressive looking older gentleman. Average height with white hair and dark eyebrows hooding fierce dark eyes. He smiled when he greeted me which made him less daunting. I sat in front of his massive desk while he settled his self.

"I was told you were adamant to see me. What can I help you with."

"I understand you presided over the hearing for a Thomas Arbaugh some years ago."

Needless to say I had his attention. "Yes, he managed to escape from the asylum."

"He's back. I have only known him as Thomas Will."

"How do you know that they are one in the same?"

"His sister, Emily, told me." He looked concerned. "Do you know of his whereabouts?"

"Yes, your honor. In fact he is three miles from here." I handed him my list.

Judge Rains picked up the telephone and spoke quietly. I didn't eavesdrop but I heard him read off Chauncey's address. Replacing the receiver, he looked at me. "Just how do you fit into all of this, Mr. Peaster." I told him of my history with, Mr. Will. Judge Rains said his case was still open. That he was in need of severe psychological treatment. "It's hard to believe he was so close. I'm surprised he would even come back to America."

"I suppose, he was ready to settle down. He wanted his sister to have everything."

"Until she ran off." He added.

"What do you remember of him from the hearing? If you don't mind my asking?"

He leaned back in his chair. "When he stood before me in that courtroom, he acted as if nothing was wrong. It wasn't until it was *recommended that he go to the asylum that he began crying. I told him he needed help realizing that what he had done was wrong. He only looked at me with spite and said, 'So I'm to pay for their sins.' He dried his tears and didn't say another word.*

Judge Rains offered me a cup of coffee. "Did he ever speak of his time working on the ships?" "No. Not to me and Emily never mentioned it." He was studying the list I'd handed him. "Do you think Emily will testify against him?" I thought about it. "I really don't know." He went back to the list. "You say you copied this out of his address book?" "Yes, your honor."

"I can tell you three people that are on this list are dead." I looked at him in horror.

"Who?"

"Sam Winston, Patty Seymour, and Mrs. Timothy Blake."

"That was the old lady who kicked Thomas and his mother out."

"Yes. She died some years back. Her butler found her in the attic. It was assumed she died of old age or a heart attack. He couldn't understand why she was up there."

"Patty." I thought. "She was Emily's friend."

"Found her a few years ago behind her apartment building. She'd been strangled."

"What about Sam Winston?"

"He was a detective. I read about it in the paper. He failed to report to work, they found him stabbed to death at his home."

I could only shake my head. "That figures, he worked the Collins case."

The judge continued. "Some of these names I haven't heard of. This isn't an address book it's a laundry list of people he's going to kill." My eyes grew large. "That explains your name being on it." Judge Rains raised an eyebrow. "Turn it over."

"He's taking his time. I'm very glad you decided to come see me."

We shook hands and I was about to leave when the phone rang. He motioned for me to stay put. He spoke quietly and hung up. "They got him." I sat down, relieved. "Evidently, he was getting ready to leave. The boys were coming out with their suitcases."

I was shaking so bad the judge offered me a glass of brandy. I drank it down and tried to get a hold of myself. "I'm going to see him. Would you like to visit with him?" I let out a relieved laugh and mopped the perspiration from my face. "By all means." He offered another brandy and I gladly took it.

Judge Rains spoke to Mr. Will, I was permitted a few minutes. He was hand cuffed to the chair. His eyes widened when I stepped inside. He softly chuckled. "Mr. Peaster."

"Yes, Mr. Will. I."

"How ungrateful you are. After all I've done for you. This will put a strain on our friendship."

"Now you can get the help you need."

"Help! You have no idea."

"Things have changed since you were a child."

"You, think so? I don't. The people I care about are still screwing me over."

"You care too much, Mr. Will. As Emily will testify."

"You think so?" He inclined his head. "I know so." I said. He sat back. "We'll see." Then he smiled. "I had high hopes for you, Mr. Peaster. Now that I think about it, you didn't last as long as Mr. Collins."

"I pity you, Mr. Will."

"How sweet of you to say."

An officer opened the door and told me I had to go. I looked at Mr. Will. "Goodbye."

"Goodbye, Mr. Peaster."

The judge and I shook hands and I made my way to the train station via the orphanage. I had to see if I could catch a glimpse of Colleen. I approached the old house. It looked as if it had seen better days. The girls were outside working in the yard. I kept my distance watching them. The ones I could see were far too old to belong to Emily. I slowly walked closer and saw two little ones with their backs to me. They were worrying over some dandelions. An older lady stepped out on the porch and called out, "Mary, Colleen. Come inside this instance!"

They stole a peek, at one another and giggled. As they walked towards the house, I could see their faces. I knew Colleen immediately. It was like seeing Emily at that age. I hurried closer, I wanted to get her attention before she disappeared. Mary had been told to go to the office while Colleen was being reprimanded on the porch. I called out. "Don't be to hard on the little one's, ma'am." They both looked my way, the lady obviously angered being interrupted. Colleen looked at me surprised then smiled.

What a little beauty she was. The lady commented that I should mind my own business and took Colleen's hand. As they turned to go inside, Colleen gave me a small wave. Soon, I thought mother and daughter would be reunited.

It's late now. Reaching the house I raced up to Emily's room and told her everything. "It's over!" She cried. I held her as she wept. "My baby is alright." I assured her she was. When she had depleted her tears she took a deep breath. "I can't decide if I'm exhausted or exhilarated."

"A good cry does that." I smiled at her. I offered her a brandy and while we drank she had me describe Colleen over and over. Satisfied over Colleen she decided that she was exhausted, as I was. I told her good night and came home.

June 5, 1920

This morning I went to her and we had breakfast. Afterwards, she asked me to take her downstairs. She placed another call to Mr. Calloway, who told her he would be ready with the documents Monday. She asked me to help her outside. I made her comfortable in a chair with a small table to prop her feet on. She breathed in the warm air. We didn't speak, merely enjoyed the day.

June 6, 1920

We were sitting at the dining table having tea after our morning outside. I, heard a carriage pulling up the drive. It, was Ida and Peeler. She looked at me with wide eyes, I held her hand. Listening, as they made their way in the back door, Ida, exclaimed. "What is this mess?" They both entered the dining room. Their stunned expres-

sions were worth a thousand words. Peeler, recovered first. "What is going on here?" He, demanded. Emily turned to him. "Having tea, Peeler. What else?" Peeler, turned his gaze towards me. "Mr. Will won't like this."

"You won't have to worry about him, any longer." I said. Ida, piped up. "Meaning what? I'd like to know!" Emily turned on her. "Don't use that tone of voice in my presence, Ida." Ida, snapped, back. "I beg your pardon!" Emily struggled to her feet. "Yes. You should beg. Both of you."

"You've no right talking to me like that you little tramp."

"How's that?"

"The way you done Mr. Will and he being so good to you. Taking care of your children even tho they weren't his. He took you back after running off the last time and you carrying on like a mad woman, cutting him when he was only trying to understand why you left him."

"Is that what he told you?"

"Yes. He was heart broken that you treated him so wrong. Then you hide in your rooms wearing that silly veil all because he slapped you and accidentally cut your cheek with his finger nail trying to calm you down. You were never a wife to him and now you're carrying on with this one behind his back."

"He told you he cut my cheek."

"Yes! A little bit of a scratch and you being so proud, you covered your face anytime he was around to remind him how he marred your beauty. I tell you I've never seen such a display of vanity. And him hurting over it, thinking he was wrong for even saying anything."

Ida, finally wound down. Emily looked at me stunned. "Where is Mr. Will?" Peeler, growled at Emily. "In jail." They, looked to one, another. "What? What for?"

"For killing our parents." Ida, spoke up. "I don't believe- your parents!" Emily held her chin high. "Yes! Ida! I was never a wife to him because I am his sister. He took care of my children because I was raped at the orphanage before he came to get me. I left because I was going to leave for good. I came back for my children because they're mine. He was furious because I had done something he had no con-

trol over and he didn't want to explain why someone would leave him. He made sure I'd never leave again." With that she motioned to her canes. "And he didn't just cut my cheek, Ida, he took my face."

She tore her veil away. Ida screamed and Peeler looked ill. "I'm not going to explain anything else to either of you. You're both fired and you will leave immediately. I will have your rooms packed up and sent to your daughter." Ida recovered and wiped at her tears. "Miss Emily, I had no-"

"I said you are dismissed." She took her chair turning her back to them. I watched them stand for a moment with weeping eyes, not fully understanding. Then they bowed their heads and left. I watched as their carriage rolled down the drive. Emily replaced her veil and looked at me smiling at her. "I've been waiting a long time for that."

"Well done." I said. "I feel like a brandy. Would you pour?" She asked. I filled two glasses and toasted her.

June 7, 1920

Emily endured another trip down stairs. She wanted to wait for Mr. Calloway. She was in an unusual mood. We ate breakfast quietly and sat in the front room. She napped as I tidied up the kitchen. Mr. Calloway arrived and she signed the documents. I witnessed, Mr. Calloway notarized and everything was wrapped up. She asked him to wait a moment before leaving and asked me to go to her room and retrieve a box she had sitting by her chaise.

She gave him instructions to wrap it and to give it to Caleb upon her demise. I saw Mr. Calloway frown at her remark but he didn't comment. She told him she appreciated his help. I showed him the door. I returned to her as she was struggling to stand up. "Where are you going?"

"Thomas' office." I escorted her inside. "Can you open those?" She used her cane to point at the file cabinets. I told her they were locked but tried anyhow.

I thought for a moment and told her I would return shortly. I went to the shed and found a crowbar. The drawer popped open without much effort. I pulled open each drawer, which were filled with paper-

work. "My goodness. He was a pack rat."Emily said as she peered.
"What are we looking for?"
"My baby's birth certificate." She said. I nodded okay.
I tried the usual method, going by last name then first name only
Mr. Will didn't file his paperwork by established routine. I ended
up back at the top drawer and rifling thru each folder. I thought of
calling Judge Rains to tell him they should come pick these up for
evidence. My first priority was finding that birth certificate.
By the third file cabinet in the bottom drawer I found the certifi-
cate. It was in a folder marked Becca. "Who in the world is Becca?" I
asked. Emily shrugged. I handed her the papers. "Good. Now I want
you to put these in a safe place until Caleb arrives." "Why didn't you
give them to Mr. Calloway?" She shook her head. "I don't trust him
with everything. You have a safe place to keep these?"
"Yes, Emily, I, do. How, did you know, he had put these in here?"
"I didn't. I only hoped he hadn't destroyed them."
"Luckily he didn't destroy them." I folded them neatly and put
them in my pocket.
"Yes." She spoke thoughtfully. "I wonder why?"
She wanted to go outside. I set up her chair and footstool. "No out
on the lawn, please. I want to feel the sun one last time." I didn't like
the way she said that but I set the chairs up like she asked. With her
situated, I relaxed beside her. "You shouldn't be morose, Emily."
"I can't help it. Things have happened so fast."
"I understand. It will get better."
"I wish the boys would come back so I could talk to them."
"They'll come home soon. Don't worry."
It was a lovely day with a slight breeze I could feel myself wanting
to doze. Emily sat quietly and without a word she removed her veil.
She tilted her head back taking in the sun. I noticed she attempted
a smile, I wanted to cry. I don't know how long we were out there. I
opened my eyes and looked in Emily's direction. My mind was playing
tricks on me as I was seeing her face as I had seen it in the photograph
she'd shown me. I blinked and she came into focus.
She was tying her veil. "Let's have a brandy." Afterwards, I carried

her upstairs. She sat on her sofa and propped her legs. "They're getting worse, Daniel." I knelt beside her. "We'll get you a good doctor." She held out her arms to me. I embraced her. "Thank you, Daniel." I kissed her forehead. "You're welcome."

    Sitting here at my desk, I look about the school room remembering. How surreal it is. I feel tired only I doubt I'll sleep. I hear a car pulling up. Maybe, it's the twins.

CHAPTER 8

CALEB BIZZLE CLOSED THE book and stubbed out his cigar. The mist had stopped and the sun was coming up. He stood and stretched and looked out the window. A beautiful morning. He gathered his shaving kit and robe and went quietly to the bathroom. He went thru his routine as if in a daze. Combing back his damp hair he looked closely at his self in the mirror. Disgusted with what he saw he turned out the light and took his things back to his room. He felt like he could use a cup of coffee. The house was still as he quietly made his way to the kitchen. Eliott was sitting at the table. He saw Caleb standing in the entry. "Coffee?" He poured out a cup not waiting for a reply. "You read it. You knew."

"Yes. You had to read it yourself." Caleb set the book on the table and picked up his coffee. "I've had a daughter this entire time, living in the same city and I never knew." He sipped his coffee and looked at Banes. "I never knew because of that bitch, Billie." "Calm down, Caleb. Let's keep our heads. I was pissed when I read it. I know this is bad."

"Bad! She kept the only woman I love away from me, denied

me my child. Emily is mutilated and you say it's bad!"

"No! It's unspeakable. Just don't do anything you'll regret."

"I wouldn't regret it."

"If you do something drastic, you won't get your daughter, that's for certain."

Bizzle rubbed his temples. "How, could she? Why, would she? How could anyone be that vindictive? I could kill her."

"Don't say that, Caleb. I know how you feel but don't say that."

They were quiet for a moment then Banes asked. "Did you have a relationship with her beyond work?"

"No! I swear. She was always attentive. I knew she liked me but I didn't lead her on."

"Okay. So, she was jealous." Banes paused. "I wonder when she may have met Thomas Will."

"Why? Do you think she knew him?"

"What reason did she have to be jealous of Emily? How did she know what Emily was there for. She could have been a client? She had to be spying for him. Keeping her messages from you. Did her behavior change.?" Bizzle shook his head.

"Maybe, we should talk to her."

"No! I never want to talk to her. I don't even want to hear her excuses for what she did."

"Okay, Caleb, okay." Banes patted his arm. Bizzle looked at him with worry. "What am I going to do? I have a daughter. How am I going to take care of her?"

"Remember, you just became executor of an estate. You'll be able to care for your daughter." Bizzle rubbed at his temples. "Emily knew something was going to happen."

"Intuition."

"I wish I could've done something."

"Stop blaming yourself, Caleb. You met a beautiful woman, you spent a couple of weeks with her. She didn't tell you very much about herself. Then she leaves. You had no idea because she didn't want you to know. She didn't really know herself, evidently.

What's done is done."

Mrs. Banes walked into the kitchen. "Good morning, boys." They told her good morning. "Oh, you've already made the coffee. I'll be right back to make your breakfast." She patted Caleb on the shoulder as she passed. When she was gone, Caleb looked at Banes. "I love your mom." He smiled. Caleb ran his fingers thru his hair. "Now I have to go about getting my daughter back, that means an attorney..."

"Aren't you forgetting?" Banes asked. "She gave Peaster the documents."

"Yes. Where, would he have put them? Should I ransack the school house and his cottage?"

"No need." Banes slid the book towards him. "You know he had this book hidden for a reason. This is an expensive journal, very well made." He flipped open the front cover and took out his pocket knife. He slid the blade along the back edge of the binding along the spine. "He guarded his book and he guarded the birth certificate." Prying up the flap Banes pulled out some papers. Handing them to Caleb. "The birth certificate."

"And the, adoption records."

Look at who is listed at the bottom." Bizzle stared at page. "She made sure you could claim her."

"Coleen Emily Bizzle. My daughter."

"All we have to do is go see a judge and get your daughter."

"We?"

"Of course. Something good had to come out of all this. I'd like to be there." Banes smiled. "Of course. Thank you." Mrs. Banes entered the kitchen, "I hope you two are hungry for pancakes." Caleb smiled. "Yes, ma'am."

"We'll leave after breakfast." Banes said.

"Not just yet. I told you I would help you with this case. I want to know what happened as much as you do."

"Oh, I think I have that figured out."

"How?"

"I'll tell you later." He poured another cup of coffee.

With breakfast over, Eliott Banes called for a squad car to meet them at Lettie's private residence and kissed his mother goodbye. Bizzle sat in the car listening to Banes.

"I told you Lettie was most happy to supply me with material that would keep Thomas Will in prison. She said she wanted to make sure he stayed there."

"You think he had something to do with Francis' death?"

"Not him."

Lettie's house was not what Bizzle expected. It was run down with chipped paint, dead tufts of grass here and there, sagging roof. They reached the door and Banes knocked. Toby answered. He was surprised to see him. "Hello, Chief." He sounded nervous. "Hello, Toby. Is your mother home?" Toby looked to his left and was about to speak when a woman's voice asked who was at the door. "Chief Banes, ma." He called back. "Let him in." Toby stepped aside. He stared at Bizzle as he passed. Lettie was on the couch in a shabby looking robe. She smiled at Banes. Bizzle could tell she was drunk. "Who is this?" She motioned at Bizzle. "This is Caleb Bizzle, Lettie, he's helping me."

"Have a seat. Would you like a drink?" They both replied, "no." She smirked. "Suit yourself."

"Where is Mr. Sheffield?" Banes asked. When Lettie didn't answer, Toby piped up. "He's gone."

"Oh. When will he be back?" Toby shrugged. "Don't know. He took Freddie and left."

"How long has he been away?"

"Right after, uh, right after Francis' funeral."

"I see. " Banes said. He was about to say something else when Lettie broke in. "I see they put that son of a bitch in jail." She waved the newspaper with Thomas Will's name in the headline. "I told you everything, chief, it helped what I told you, didn't it?"

"Oh yes, it helped immensely. That's not why I'm here." Bizzle noticed her nervous demeanor, she kept looking at Toby who was still standing by the door. Bizzle slowly eased over to stand by him. Pretending to look at the bric a brac on a table.

"Well, I don't know what else I can tell you, Chief."

"As you've probably heard, Thomas Will's house burned down." Lettie began to cackle. "Isn't that a shame?"

"Tell me, Lettie, what did Francis die of?" Lettie stopped laughing tears sprang in her eyes. "Wha.. She died,,,of a fever."

"What caused the fever, Lettie?" She sniffed and looked for something to blow her nose. "Doc, couldn't say."

"It's lucky it wasn't contagious." Banes continued. "I've spoken with the doctor, Lettie."

"Oh."

"He said, he'd seen, similar symptoms in some of the girls that have worked for you."

"Francis was never there." She barked. "Francis didn't know anything about it."

"She was there one time. I'd figure a week or so before she died."

"I don't know what you're talking about."

"She was pregnant and she aborted."

"No! She had a fever is all."

"Because of the abortion."

"No! No, no, no." Lettie bellowed.

"Leave my mother alone. It was Reginal and Phil." Toby clamped his mouth shut.

"What do you know about it, Toby?"

"Don't, you say a word, Toby." Lettie warned him.

"Lettie, I know you had a woman working for you who performed abortions when the girls got into trouble. The doctor knows her. He treated the girls when they became ill. Only Francis didn't say anything right away, did she? She didn't think she was that ill. It was too late for the doctor to do anything for her."

Lettie bawled. "Francis, my poor Francis. Those boys attacked her." Toby was consoling her. "I know Lettie." Banes said. Toby looked up. "You should go. Can't you see she's suffering?"

"Not just yet. You see we still have to figure out who killed the twins."

Toby seethed. "Serves them right and that awful Mr. Peaster, always leering at Francis. He made me sick."

"Those three." Lettie cried, "deserved to die in that fire." Banes nodded. "Well, your wrong there. Only one died in the fire." They looked at Banes quizzically.

"Peaster and the twins were already dead before the fire got them." Toby stood erect. "There were four people in that house."

"Four?" Toby exclaimed. "No it was only,,," He was quiet. "No. The paper said that those three." He was lost for words.

"No, Toby. The paper said, that we found three bodies burned in the fire."

"How do you know the fire didn't get them?" Lettie said.

"When we found Peaster, he had a knife handle sticking out of his chest. The twins had their heads bludgeoned with, what we figure, an axe." Toby stared at Banes. "I noticed that the axe is missing from the school house. You used to chop wood for Mr. Peaster, didn't you Toby?"

He only stared. Lettie stood up. "Wait a minute. Who was the fourth person, your talking about?"

"Emily Will." Lettie was stunned. "What? I thought she was away at a sanitarium."

"No. She was upstairs in her room. She couldn't get out because she was crippled. I wonder, Toby, if you could tell me the whereabouts of that axe."

"She didn't call out. I didn't,,," Lettie slapped his face. "Shut up. You fool." Banes grabbed Lettie's arm as she was about to slap him again. "Sit down, Lettie." He pushed her onto the couch. "That's enough." Toby had tears streaming down his cheeks. He looked to Bizzle and back at Banes. "I swear, chief, I didn't know. If she had called out, I would have gotten her."

He collapsed on the sofa. Banes sat down on the coffee table and soothingly said. "Tell me what happened, Toby."

Toby wiped his eyes on his shirt sleeve. "I noticed Francis wasn't acting herself. She always seemed on the verge of tears. I tried to talk to her, but she would only say that, she would be alright. She got sick and I sat by her bed one day telling her about school. She began crying and said she didn't want to hear about school. The next day, Mr. Peaster asked how she was feeling. I told him she was miserable. At that moment Reginal and Phillip looked at one another and smiled. After school, I asked her, had they done something? She wouldn't answer me. She didn't have to.

I over heard the doctor talking to ma when she was worse and I knew then what had happened. I waited for them to come back. I checked, everyday, to see if the car was in the drive. The night they did return Mr. Will wasn't with them. They parked outside Peaster's house. I looked thru the window and they were arguing. Then Reginal grabbed Peaster and pinned his arms behind him. Phil punched him several times. Peaster sunk to the floor.

Reginal pulled him up and slammed his head against the door several times. I saw the blood on the door and it was running down his face. Afterwards, they each grabbed an arm and dragged him to the house. I followed. They weren't worried if anyone was about. All I could hear them say was they were going to let him see his lover one last time.

I ran back to the school and grabbed the axe. When I reached the house, the door was standing open. It looked like Peaster was fighting back. They only laughed. Reginal pulled a knife and stabbed at him. Phil was laughing. I snuck up behind him and sunk the axe in. He fell to his knees and on over once I wrenched it out. Reginal didn't see what was going on he was bent over Peaster after he had stabbed him the last time and was watching him gasp. I came up behind him and repeated the deed. He grabbed at his head and rocked about.

He hit the floor with a thud. I had to put my foot on his neck to pry the axe out. After that I smashed the lamps and the flames grew fast. I heard Peaster call me. I knelt down by him. 'Don't let me burn.' Was all he could manage, to say. I dragged him as far as I could until the smoke was so thick, I couldn't breath. I realized he was dead so I just ran and didn't stop until I got home."

"So, you didn't hear Emily Will call for help."

"No, sir."

Banes nodded then went to the door and called in an officer. "Toby Sheffield, you are under arrest for the murder of Reginal Will, Phillip Will and Emily Will." The officer cuffed Toby as Banes read him his rights. "No!!!!" Lettie screamed. She tried to push her way to Toby. "You can't do this, Chief, after what they did to my Francis." Banes held her back as Toby was led outside. "He's all I have. Please." She hung onto Banes arm until he wrestled it away from her. She crawled after Bizzle and Banes onto the porch. Toby was in the police car.

Toby didn't struggle as she banged on the window, pleading. Banes and Bizzle waited until the squad car pulled away before following. Out of sight Bizzle spoke up. "Kinda rough on her."

"Don't feel bad. She ran that whore house for years. She didn't seem to concerned about those girls lives. What goes around."

"She turned over information on Thomas Will."

"Out of spite. I don't feel sorry for her. Now we know what happened." Bizzle looked out the window, thinking. *"Now we know."*

CHAPTER 9

THEY DROVE IN SILENCE to the station. With Toby booked and processed and signing the confession he'd written, Banes and Bizzle went to the house. Inside, they were taking their coats off when Banes asked, "Do you have anymore of that scotch, left?" Bizzle smiled meekly. "Sure."

Eliott sipped his drink at the kitchen table. Mrs. Banes had gone to bed. Caleb lighted a cigar and let out a long breath. "I'm curious. How come you never did anything about Lettie's before?"

"It was licensed. Never had any complaints about the place. Of all the complaints I'd heard in my short time here not once did they complain about that place. He had quite the empire built from what she told me. He used his barges to import liquor from Canada and Mexico. Of course, his ships brought in rum from Jamaica."

"He was never caught?"

"He paid off the inspector's. He spent a fortune in pay offs to get his liquor in. This was prime stuff and he appreciated the best.

So did his clientele. They didn't have to worry that it was aged in a bath tub. Plus, they had access to the girls. Speaking of which, while you were away at the lawyer's office I was interested in Peaster's description of those woods he traversed.

I decided to go over there and take a walk myself and see just what he was always tripping over. Those woods are dense, I don't know how he didn't break a leg traipsing around. I found a kind of path he'd forged and followed it. I could make out the highs and lows of the ground it did seem as if there could be graves like he thought."

"You didn't see anything suspicious?"

"No. I imagine when it's dark and in the shape Peaster was in you could imagine all sorts of things. I did wonder what became of the girls, Mr. Will spoke of. Was he trying to frighten Peaster or was he serious. On I walked and ended up coming out at Lettie's. It was quiet that time of the day, I stood there remembering the journal.

Then I saw a man backing out the door. It was Darby, who worked there. I approached him. "Morning, Darby." He turned to me. "Well, mornin' Chief. What brings you out this way?"

I told him I had a few questions to ask. "Go right ahead." He tells me.

"What dealings did you have with Mr. Will?"

"Oh, all sorts, I put his carriage away then his car. Served drinks, cleaned up, you know." He laughed.

"What do you know about the woods between here and Mr. Will's?" He shrugged. "What happened to the girls?"

"What do you mean?"

"When they were hurt?"

"None hurt that I know of."

I tried to throw him off. "I have it on good authority that there are bodies buried in those woods." He looked at me indifferently, "Most likely."

"So you know who's buried there."

"Not by name."

"Did you help bury them?"

"No." He laughed. "I wasn't even born yet." I asked him what he meant.

"My mama told me that was a cemetery when she was little. Nobody tended the graves, they all grew over, with time." I asked him how old he thought the graves were.

"No tellin'. Mama said when she was little the flu hit around these parts, lotta folks died."

I figured I'd made a fool of myself long enough until he chimed in. "What? You think Mr. Will kill girls and bury them?" I told him no. "That's what Mr. Peaster wanted." I looked at him and he continued. "Yeah. He was always, all the time, beggin' Mr. Will to help him." I asked with what. He rolled his eyes, "Get rid of the girls."

"You told me they didn't get hurt." He shook his head. "They weren't hurt. They were dead." "So, I flat out ask him how they ended up dead." He took a step closer to me. "That Mr. Peaster got mean when he drank. If they didn't do what he wanted he would always yell that, it pissed him off, when he paid someone good money for a job and they did it poorly.

"What did he do?" I asked. He said, "He strangle them."

"Good night." Bizzle sputtered. "It was true, then."

"From what Darby says. I asked how Mr. Will helped. He said, 'He put them in crates on the barge and dump them.' I was amazed. I asked how he knew. 'I went with him. Shove 'em off in the water when nobody was looking.' I told him he could be in a lot of trouble. He just shrugged. 'How's that? You don't have no proof.' Little bastard laughed again. 'Yeah. That Mr. Will was smart.'

"I was desperate. I told him I could talk to the crews, someone had to see something. He only looked at me, knowing. 'They don't know what's in them crates.' Then he turned to go and stopped. 'Can I go now?' I hated the little mocking jerk but I told him yes. He knew I didn't have anyway of proving what he'd told me."

"Horrible. To think that Emily was on friendly terms with that man."

"He was all she had. Evidently, he didn't believe Mr. Will since he couldn't remember anything of what he did."

Bizzle refilled their glasses. "On to better subjects. What are you going to do after you get Colleen?"

"I've been thinking about that. I don't want her to grow up in Carthage. There's too many memories. I've been thinking of starting fresh out in California."

"That sounds good. I'm thinking of leaving here, myself."

"Sure. You could get on the police force out there."

"No. No. I'm thru with police work. This last ordeal was the final straw for me. I saw to much during the war and with all that has happened. I can't do it anymore. I have plenty of money saved up. I could buy some land and, I don't know, grow oranges, lettuce, anything, something. I need a change. I know that the weather would help mom."

"We should go together. Help each other."

"Why, would you need, help? You're a rich man, now."

"True. I've never had a family. And with my daughter, I'm sure your mom would be a great help to me."

"I suppose. I'll have to think about it."

Feeling fatigued Bizzle stretched. "Do think about it, Eliott. I'm going to get Colleen in the morning."

"I'll be there." Banes said.

Bizzle smiled. "Don't worry, I'm not going to do anything to Billie."

Caleb Bizzle sat on his bed holding the picture of Emily. "I'm going to get our daughter, tomorrow, Emily. Help me, be a good father. I'll tell her about you all the time and what you did to protect her. When she's old enough, I'll let her read Peaster's journal. She should know." Bizzle fought his tears and lost. "I'll never forget you, Emily. I loved you and I will love you, forever. What a life we could have had." He curled up on the bed clutching the teddy bear he would give his daughter.

CHAPTER 10

SITTING AND WAITING FOR Judge Rains, Eliott Banes smiled as he watched Caleb Bizzle fidget in his chair. Bizzle had called Judge Rains since he was familiar with Thomas and Emily. Rains told him there shouldn't be a problem but wanted to see him nonetheless. The door opened and Judge Rains walked in. He greeted Banes and Bizzle and asked them into his chambers.

"I have the papers for Colleen, if you'd like to see them, your honor." Bizzle nervously held them out. Judge Rains smiled at his anxiety. He looked them over. "This is fine." He folded them and handed them back. "I know something of what happened. Tell me about Emily."

Bizzle explained what he knew of her.

"So, in all that time you only knew her as Emily Will."

"Well, yes. As I said Thomas' last name was Arbaugh. I imagine he coerced Emily to take the Will name." The judge thought for a moment. "So, he didn't know." Bizzle looked concern. "Know what?"

"This Emily, had a secret of her own." He looked at Bizzle, thoughtfully. "Judge, please, what do you mean?"

"Thomas Arbaugh's sister, Emily Arbaugh, wasn't quite two months old when she died, at the orphanage." Banes and Bizzle looked at one another. "What?" They both said.

"There was another girl, an Emily Morgan, who disappeared at the time indicated." Bizzle began rubbing his temples. "This is incredible."

"I'm sorry you had to find out this way. I thought you should know." Banes spoke up. "You know, I remember reading in the journal, when she was talking to Peaster, that she didn't even know she had a brother, until he wrote to her."

"Yes." The judge said. Bizzle looked up. "If the name on the letter was Emily Arbaugh , wouldn't Emily Morgan see the difference?"

"Chauncey!" Banes exclaimed. "He worked there. He probably had something to do with it." Bizzle sat back. "Why would she go along with it? Especially, when he told her they would go by the name Will. Wouldn't she see that they weren't related?"

Banes shrugged. "Maybe she did. You read it yourself, she was miserable at that place. By the time he showed up she'd been raped, was pregnant, and totally alone. All she had, were promises. She didn't know how he would act. It was her chance for something better. So, she kept quiet and went along with whatever he said."

"She must have resembled Thomas' mother, at least what he remembered, enough to make him think there was nothing wrong." Judge Rains said. "Poor, child." Banes faced the judge. "What of Emily Morgan's parents. Any relation of hers out there?"

"Not that we, know of. She was found on the steps of the orphanage. A note pinned to her with her name on it. There were some inquiries, nothing came of it." He looked at Bizzle. "I hope I haven't distressed you, telling you this." Bizzle chuckled. "No, your honor, in fact I'm glad that my daughter isn't related to that Arbaugh clan in any way." Judge Rains and Banes looked relieved.

"Speaking of your daughter." Banes reminded him. Bizzle nodded. "Let's go."

CHAPTER 11

BIZZLE CLUTCHED THE TEDDY bear as he waited. A Miss Lydecker went to get Colleen. He stood when he heard them approaching. She walked around the corner holding Colleen's hand. She tugged at her to keep up. "C'mon Colleen." Bizzle didn't like her handling Colleen in that manner. "There is someone here who wants to meet you."

Shyly, Colleen peeked around Miss Lydecker's skirt. Bizzle saw the auburn hair and the bright green eyes peering at him. He caught his breath, kneeling, he held out his hand. "Hello, Colleen." She looked at him, square in the eyes. "Hello." She spoke clearly and took a step closer.

Bizzle brought around the teddy bear. "I have something for you." Colleen brightened. "For me?"

Bizzle nodded. She timidly took the bear and looked at it. She traced the face just as Emily had done. Then she smiled. "Thank you."

Bizzle gushed, "You're welcome. Will you sit with me?" She nodded and followed him not taking her eyes off the bear. "Do you like it here, Colleen?" She looked at him then at Miss

Lydecker. "Could we have a moment?" Miss Lydecker took a step back at his serious tone. She turned and left the room.

"Now. You can tell me, she's gone." Colleen looked about the room again to make sure. She shook her head. "Would you like to live someplace else?" She nodded emphatically. Bizzle smiled. "Would you like to live with me?" She shook her head. "I don't know you."

"I know. It's a long story, Colleen. I'm your father. I've come to take you away from here."

She studied him intently. "Daddy?"

"Yes. I've been looking for you."

"You're my daddy?"

"Yes, baby."

"Where is my mama?" Her tone was serious. "She's in heaven, honey." She frowned. "Why?"

"I think you're too young to understand but in time I'll tell you all about it."

"Are you coming back?"

"I had thought that if you came with me, neither one of us will have to come back."

She toyed with the bear's ear and looked about the room then she steadied her gaze on Bizzle. She stared at him awhile. Bizzle felt uneasy, what she would say. "Never come back?"

"Never."

"You promise?"

"Honey, I swear." She studied him. "Alright." She smiled at him. His throat tightened seeing how she resembled Emily in gesture. "Good. Is there anything you want to get before we go?" She thought for a moment. "No." He held out his arms and she gave him a hug. "Can I call you daddy?" Thru his tears, Bizzle told her, "Please."

Judge Rains and Chief Eliott Banes waited on the steps outside the orphanage. Soon, the door opened and Bizzle stepped out looking proud. "Gentlemen, I would like for you to meet my daughter, Colleen Emily Bizzle." They each said hello to her, she smiled and hid her face in Bizzle's shoulder. They laughed. "She's a little shy."

"I'm glad things worked out for you, Mr. Bizzle." Miss Lydecker was standing behind them. "Yeah, thank you Miss Lydecker. We'll be going now." Bizzle went down the steps with the judge and Banes. She called out, "Goodbye, Colleen." Colleen stiffened at her voice. "Bye,,, you mean ole bat." She called back. Banes snickered. "She's not that shy."

They were on their way back when Judge Rains said he was curious about something. "What's that, your honor?" The judge paused. "I don't want you to get upset, Caleb, in fact, I don't want you to come." Bizzle turned to look at him. "Eliott and I were talking while you were inside. We want to speak to Chauncey."

Bizzle smiled at Colleen, who was intent on every word. "Sure. Drop us off and we'll have some lunch and some ice cream." Colleen clapped her hands. "Yeah!" Banes pulled over and let them out in front of a restaurant. Banes leaned over. "See you, in little while." Bizzle waved them off.

CHAPTER 12

JUDGE RAINS AND CHIEF Banes stood on the porch of Chauncey's house. Banes knocked on the door. He heard a gruff voice say come in. He slowly opened the door. It was dark inside with all the shades drawn. An odor of sweat and bad cooking leeched out. The judge made a face and put his handkerchief to his nose. Banes got his gag reflex under control while letting his eyes adjust to the dark.

"What do you want?" The voice snarled.

"Arnold Chauncey?"

"Yeah."

"I'm Chief Eliott Banes and this is Judge Harold Rains."

"What's that to me?"

"We would like to speak with you if you have a moment."

"Well, come in and close the door. Were you raised in a barn?" Banes hated to shut off their only supply of fresh air. He turned to see the creature sitting legless in a ratty wheelchair. What little bit of hair he had was still red and the leering face as he imagined. So this is what had his hands on Emily, Banes thought. "I'm waiting, boy. What do you want?"

"I wanted to discuss, Emily Will."

"What of it?"

"She's dead."

"Thank you. You can let yourself out." He put his hands on the wheels as if to roll away.

"Wait a minute. Your sons are dead as well."

"I already know that. Say, you're the guy that investigated the fire."

"Yes."

"So you come all this way to tell me something I already know."

"No." Banes, was getting flustered. Judge Rains, interjected. "We wanted to understand about your time at the orphanage. We know that Emily Will was really Emily Morgan." Chauncey began laughing. "Yeah. I put one over good on that little punk."

"You knew Thomas Will."

"He's my nephew. Only he doesn't know that. His mother and I were half brother and sister. My old man was a Chauncey, her's was a Will. We went to work for Arbaugh at the same time. He didn't like the way I did things so he fired me. I kept my eye on her tho. I knew about Thomas. Went by every now and then to see him. I never spoke to him but when they dragged him into the asylum I knew who he was.

"Did you ever tell him you were his uncle?" Banes asked.

"Nah. Never, told."

"What happened to him at the asylum?" Judge Rains asked.

"I didn't think he would last, considering how weak, his mother was. He was tougher than I thought. He only got whipped by the other boys, once. Actually, a lucky punch took him down. The next time was different. He never provoked a fight but he never backed down and he always finished them. He got me in trouble with so many of the boys being sent to the infirmary. My bosses told me to handle it, so I did.

Sometimes, I was in charge of sitting outside the hell hole. It was down in the bowels of the building where they kept the really violent men. They only existed down in that, hole. The only air and light were small barred openings about twenty feet up the walls. Summer, winter, burnin' up or freezin' to death.

The stench was terrible, even with the room and the inmates hosed down every week. They'd get about a dozen of us with whips and bats to keep them up against the wall while they were washing. All the piss and vomit and anything else, even the rotten food, they lowered down everyday, would be washed down the sewer grate. Didn't matter, by the next day it would smell just as bad as if it'd never been done.

Sometimes, we'd get a hard case that thought he was tough. It wouldn't be until the next hosing that his body would be found. I thought that since locking ole Thomas in the broom closet for two days didn't tame him, I'd see how he liked being stuck with them for a night."

The judge wiped a tear away. Banes, lowered his head. Chauncey, continued.

"When I dragged him out next morning, I thought he was dead. There was so much blood and muck on his little naked body. I put him in the big sink basin and washed him off. He came around from the fresh pain of his cuts being scrubbed. I dressed him and put him in his bunk. My bosses were happy with the change in him and told me to keep up the good work. It took him a good month or better for him to heal up.

When he was able to get back to doin' his chores, I thought havin' 'im mop up the sitting area outside the hell hole would be a good reminder to him. It never took him long to mop and get out of there, let me tell you." Chauncey, chuckled remembering. "He'd been there almost a year. I thought everything was going smooth, he was as good as gold. But, that little bastard was planning the whole time.

One night, out of the blue, he provoked a fight. I hauled him up and told him, 'some people just never learn.' Back to the hell hole we went. He struggled the whole way. Once I got the door unlocked was when he turned. He elbowed me in the gut and then kicked me in the balls. I doubled over in pain that was when he shoved me thru the door.

He used my keys to unlock the window. I was watching him thru the little window in the door. I hollered at him to give me back those keys. He dragged a chair over and stood on it, holding the keys in front of my eyes. By then, I'd made so much noise the men were stirring behind me. I growled at him to give me those keys. He only smiled. I was being dragged back from the door, then he dropped the keys.

Out the window and into the night, he disappeared. I was found the next day, either it was luck or he'd planned it, when they came to hose the cell. I was fired from there so I went to work at, Mrs. Tuttle's. I used to pass the time at night reading, the girls, files. That was how I learned little Emily had died. Years later, I was going thru the mail and I saw a letter addressed to, Emily Arbaugh.

We had a Emily Morgan there. She favored Kathleen enough. I read the letter and thought I'd have a little fun."

"So, you put her name on the envelope." Banes said.

"Yep. And, the rest is history."

"How did you come to contact, Thomas, after so long?" Banes asked.

"How do you mean?"

"You were blackmailing him."

"Oh that. It was a while after. I kept an eye on Emily. Didn't know when he'd be comin' for her. It was a long time, tho. She got more sad as the years dragged. One day she went into town to run Mrs. Tuttle's errands. When she returned, she was happy. She went on about her business but I could tell something was up. I lost a lot of sleep watching her.

The next week, she leaves to run her errands, as usual. I followed her that time. Found her sitting at the train station, crying. Then, outta nowhere he comes running towards her. Grabs her and gets her on the train. I was the only one who knew what he looked like. I asked the porter where the train was headed. I decided to follow. Once I was down there, I saw his house and asked around about him.

Lotta folks, sang his praises. I knew he was gonna stick around there for awhile, so I came back. I'd know where to find him if I had to. A few years passed and I left, Mrs. Tuttle's. Decided to try my hand on the river barges. I, hired on with his outfit. I worked them a couple of months when I saw him and another man with a girl climb on board. "

"Collins!" Banes said. Chauncey shrugged. "Don't know the name. I was asleep on deck one night, hunkered down between the crates. I heard a commotion and peeked around to see. I seen him choke that man to death then just tossed him in the river."

"What about the girl?" Banes asked.

"I didn't see what happened to her. I jumped ship and called the police."

"You called the police?"

"Sure. Shake him up a little. I wanted to see if he could lie his way out of it." Chauncey was quiet for a moment. "I guess he did, I didn't hear nothin' about it."

"That's the leverage you had on him."

"Yeah. Couldn't have come at a better time. It was a couple months later. I was at a bar, drinking. Had a little too much. When I went to cross the street, I walked right in front of a car. I laid there quite awhile before anyone found me."

"You mean the driver didn't stop?"

"No. Come to think of it. They did what they could at the hospital, gangrene set in, and they cut 'em off."

"So, you get in touch with Thomas and told him you'd turn him in."

"Yeah. He was surprised to hear from me. He did what I said. Even brought my boys to see me. They were strange, I'll have to admit. Musta got it from their mama."

The judge was still the entire time. Banes just shook his head. "Why did you drag Emily into the situation?"

"Why not. Nothin' else to do. I heard she had another kid."

"Yes. The father has her now."

"What's her name?"

"I don't think you need to know that."

"Why not? If I hadn't stepped in he wouldn't have a daughter now, would he?"

"You're vile. They were to be married, they could've been happy."

"And yet her fate ended the same way. Pregnant and living with a maniac and no one to help her."

"You sound like you feel sorry for her."

"Not really. She was a tease."

"Shut your mouth." Judge Rains cried.

"Get out of my house."

The Judge and Banes rose. "If you see, Caleb, tell him I said hello." Banes blanched. On the porch and in fresh air, Banes shut the door on the contemptible figure. Banes saw the judge wipe his nose and eyes. "Judge?" Banes asked. He shook his head and squared his shoulders. "I had no idea what went on in that place."

"Do you think it's changed?"

"I don't know. I thought they would help him. Only a killer was produced."

Banes patted the old man on the shoulder. "We better go pick up Caleb."

"Don't tell him about this. Please." Rains implored. Banes thought and nodded.

CHAPTER 13

THEY WERE DROPPING THE judge back to his office saying their goodbye's, when a newspaper reporter noticed, Bizzle. "Hey... Caleb Bizzle," He greeted. "You're a sight for sore eyes." Bizzle shook his hand. "How are you, Morton?" Morton looked at Coleen. "Oh, same old thing. Say who is this little beauty?"

"This is my daughter, Coleen. Say 'hi' to Morton, Coleen." She whispered, 'hi'. Morton shook her little hand. "I didn't know you had a kid."

"Neither did I till a few days ago."

"Say you missed a lot going on around here. Did you hear about that Thomas Arbaugh fellow being apprehended?"

"I, sure did. "

"I was the one who got the exclusive from the fellow who turned him in."

"Good for you."

"Say. Now that I think about it, he mentioned you being involved with that fellows, sister." Bizzle, looked at him. He could tell the gears were churning in Morton's head. "Is this?" Bizzle nodded. "Well. I have to get an interview. Just the thing. Father and daughter reunited."

"Wipe your mouth, Morton." Morton wiped at his mouth then stopped. "Ha Ha. Come on, just tell me what you're going to do now."

"I... er, we, rather, are going to California."

"I don't blame ya, Not one bit. Where exactly?"

"Maybe, Los Angeles and see how we like it. We need to get going. Going shopping."

"Wonderful. Good to see you again. Nice to meet you, little one." Morton patted her head, Colleen made a face. Bizzle situated Colleen in the car between him and Banes. "Hurry, he'll have all of them chasing us." Banes stepped on the gas. They found a department store and a very eager sales lady waited on them. She helped pick out a complete new wardrobe for Colleen from hats to shoes and everything in between. Colleen liked the attention and the pretty dresses but Bizzle noticed she was getting tired.

Once the last package was brought up to Caleb's apartment, Banes collapsed in a chair. "How, do women do it. I've never been this tired. How can something as simple as buying clothes exhaust a body?" Bizzle laughed. "I know what you mean. I'm going to put her down." Colleen's eyes were half closed already. Banes got up and kissed her forehead. "I'm happy for you, Bizzle."

Caleb returned with a bottle of, scotch. "To celebrate the day, my friend." Banes nodded with approval. Banes sipped his drink. "So, when do you plan to go to California?"

"Tonight."

"So soon?"

"Yeah. I have to, Eliott. I'm leaving late tonight. Hopefully, I won't run into anybody at three in the morning."

"What about all your things?"

"This apartment came furnished. All I have, are my clothes."

"What about your office."

"Nothing Earl and Lyle can't handle. I called Earl this morning and told him what happened and to fire Billie."

"Oh, boy."

"So." Bizzle inclined his head to Banes.

"So, what?" Banes replied.

"Have you thought about coming along?"

"Yes. I spoke to mom about it last night after you went to bed. She said she would love to help you with the baby. I think she's excited to have a little one, running around. She perked up, considerably."

"Wonderful. It'll be nice to have friends in a new place."

"It may take awhile. I have to clear up some things and let the town council find a replacement. I don't think it will be too long before we can join you."

"Sure. By then I'll have a house set up. " Banes stood and pulled on his coat. Bizzle extended his hand. "I want to thank you, Eliott." Banes shook his hand. "Don't mention it. Call me when you get settled."

"I will. Give my love to your mom." Banes nodded and closed the door. Bizzle, looked in on Colleen. She was sleeping, deeply. He couldn't quite get over the fact that she was his, now. She was perfect in every way. He lingered in the door way until the phone rang. "Hello."

"Caleb, it's Earl. Look I can't talk very long but I wanted to tell you, she's gone."

"Good. " Caleb said. "I have to go. " Earl hurried. " Come by the office tonight."

"I am. I need to clean out my desk." They hung up.

Caleb picked up the receiver and dialed the train ticket office. He made his reservation on the three fifteen to Los Angeles. He quietly took his suitcase and clothes to the living room, to not wake Colleen. His duffle bag was inside when he opened it. Looking at all the packages stacked about he decided to pack his things in the duffle and use the suitcase for her clothes. Setting aside a clean suit of clothes for himself, he began unwrapping the boxes from the department store.

He smiled, laying the tiny articles carefully inside. He picked out a pretty blue dress, for her to wear, on the train. He took a

shower and shaved and was fastening his trousers when Colleen
awakened. She rubbed her eyes and looked around the room.
"Did you have a nice nap, baby?" She looked towards Bizzle and
smiled. "Daddy." She stretched her arms out to him. He kissed
her cheek and rubbed her back. "How would you like to put on
one of your pretty dresses and go have dinner?" She nodded en-
thusiastically. Bizzle ran the tub for her and helped her bathe.

He was awkward brushing her hair but he got thru it without to many complaints. Colleen preened for him once she was
dressed. She stared at her new shoes admirably. She was a little
lady at dinner. Bizzle was in awe of her manners. An older couple
complimented her dress and hat, she smiled warmly and thanked
them.

There was still time and they walked around looking at the
store display windows. He told her they were going to California
and all the things they would do out there. Bizzle felt nervous
with her but Colleen was completely at ease. "When we get out
there, Mr. Banes and his mother are going to come and stay with
us." She giggled. "I like Mr. Banes. He's funny."

"You'll like his mom, as well. She's very sweet." Bizzle saw a
pay phone and called the office, there was no answer. "Oh well,
they'll show up sooner or later." He told her "Would you like to
see where I used to work?" She nodded.

He flipped on the lights and looked around. "C'mon." Colleen
followed him to his office. "How come you don't work here, anymore, daddy?" Bizzle smiled. "Because, I got a new job, taking
care of you." Bizzle sat down behind his desk and pulled the trash
can close. Tossing out unimportant bits he closed the drawers.
Pulling open the middle drawer, he found a key. He frowned.

He heard the commotion outside then Lyle and Earl strolled
in. "Hey, stranger." Lyle said and shook Bizzle's hand. "What a
day." He continued then paused when he saw Colleen. "My, my,
my." He knelt in front of her. "How do you do? My name is Lyle."
She smiled at him and said "I'm Colleen. He's my daddy." Lyle
chuckled.

"Earl, come and meet my daughter." Earl shook her little hand. "It's very nice to meet you." Colleen stared at the floor. "Nice to meet you." She whispered. Earl motioned to Lyle, Lyle took the hint. "Hey, Colleen, lets go outside and see if we can find some candy in the other desk."

"Okay." She took Lyle's hand. When they were out of ear shot, Earl turned to Caleb. "Boy, did you miss a show. After you called me, I called him and told him the whole story. We met up here. She, was at her desk, as usual. Lyle, had the most fun, telling her you had called. She was mad as a hornet that you hadn't called her personally. 'Wait, till I get a hold of him.' She says then Lyle lowers the boom. He tells her she's fired and why she's fired.

Once, he finished telling her, she got real quiet. Without a word she steps out back and comes in with a box. She slammed a few things around on her desk then grabs her purse and walks out.

"Good riddance. I hope you two can find another secretary." Bizzle said.

"Don't worry about us. What are you going to do?"

"I'm taking Colleen to Los Angeles, tonight."

Tonight! What time?"

"The three fifteen." Earl looked at his watch. "It's almost one thirty. I didn't realize the time. She ought to be in bed."

"She had a long nap. She'll sleep on the train."

"How's she taking to you?"

"Like a duck to water. I'm the one who's nervous." Earl, chuckled. " She's gonna be a heartbreaker."

Caleb smiled. "Won't she, tho. My friend, Eliott and his mother are going to stay with us. I can certainly use the help."

"That'll be good for her."

Lyle and Colleen walked back into the room both chewing on gum they managed to scrounge. She stood by Caleb as Lester spoke. "Here's the evening paper." Caleb glanced at it. "Didn't take Morton very long to knock that out."

"I read the story that, that Peaster character gave. Whatever happened to that old guy that was blackmailing ole Will?"

"I don't know. Eliott and Judge Rains went to talk to him. I had no desire to know what he had to say and didn't bother asking."

"Fair enough." Lyle said. Bizzle had his mind on the key in his pocket. "I wonder if you two would do me a favor."

"Sure." Earl agreed.

"I have one last thing to do. Would you watch her?" I'll only be twenty minutes or so."

They, eyed one another and nodded.

CHAPTER 14

Billie, shivered as she finished packing her new clothes in the two trunks she had purchased. Thinking she heard a noise, she stood very still. Nothing. Letting out a relieved breath, she checked the door. Feeling silly she returned to her bedroom to pack. She had a couple hours before her train.

She, re-read the evening paper. The picture showed her Caleb and little Colleen. She favored Emily, Billie thought. Reading that he planned on Los Angeles, Billie called the station to confirm his reservation. She was told that two adjoining compartments were held on the three fifteen. She hung up and waited a few minutes then called to reserve her own compartment.

Somehow she would make Caleb understand why she did those things. She loved him more than ever, if he would only listen. She smirked, thinking of Thomas. Sitting cuffed to his chair when she went to him. She had gotten his call right after a little man named Calloway asked to see Caleb. She told him he was expected anytime, he told her he would wait.

She was on the phone with Thomas when Caleb walked in. She begged off so Caleb wouldn't hear and hurrying into his office, she rushed welcoming him back. She left without a thought to Calloway. Sitting across from Thomas, she smiled at his predicament. "I saw the paper this morning. I wondered if you would call."

Thomas ignored her jibe. "I need the money, Billie."

"For what? You're sunk."

"I need the money and a good attorney." He snarled.

"Seems like a waste to me. You're not getting out."

"Don't mess around."

"You don't have much to say about it."

"I'm warning you."

"You see what all your need to control has caused." She dropped the newspaper in front of him. "Your poor sister, how could you?" Thomas smiled at her. "You wanted Caleb."

Billie's face reddened. "Not at that price."

Thomas, chuckled. "Everybody gets a conscience all of a sudden. First Collins, then Peaster and now you. You make me sick."

"The feeling is mutual." Billie said thru gritted teeth.

"Of course, you wouldn't act so superior, if not for my position. Seeing Thomas Will vulnerable makes people, bold."

"I think it will be good for you. Maybe paying your debt will humble you."

"Being humble didn't attract your attention, now did it?"

"It's different now."

"You failed me, Billie."

"I did what you asked."

"You know the first thing Emily will do is contact him."

"I can't help that now."

He smiled. "No. But, I, can." She shivered. "I have to go."

"Don't do this, Billie." She left him with the newspaper.

Her legs were weak walking out of the station. When she made the last step, outside she rested against the railing. Drying her eyes, she checked the time. She had to get back.

It was unusually quiet back at the office. Caleb's door was open, he was gone. She found his note crumpling it she thought.

'He's gone to her.' The next day, she read that Thomas' house had burned down. She thought it funny that what goes around, comes around. She went to work, everyday, hoping to hear from Caleb. Only, Earl received the call.

Those two old flatfoots standing at her desk, smiling. Lyle telling her with glee everything that had happened and how they all agreed that she was no longer needed. To hell with them she thought as she stormed out. Her first stop was the bank to empty the safe deposit box.

It was a few years, of knowing one another before Thomas gave her a key. "In case of an emergency," he told her. He warned her not to get to curious about the contents. That he had a contact in the bank who would call him if anything should happen.

'Well,' she thought, 'he can't come to the phone, right now." Either, his contact was out that day or he was lying, because the clerk didn't blink when she asked for the box. She waited while the clerk unlocked the safe. They both turned their respective keys and the clerk withdrew the box for her. She was seated in a private room and left alone.

She shook her head seeing all the money lying there. It took her awhile to count out the stacks of twenties. Soon, she had four hundred thousand dollars piled up. She crammed her purse full and left the key on the table. On her way home she saw two trunks sitting in the display window. Those would do, she thought.

The taxi driver loaded them into the trunk and was handsomely rewarded for his trouble of bringing them up to her apartment. He tipped his hat and whistled as he gazed at the two crisp bills she handed him. She began taking her clothes out of the closet to pack and stopped. 'Time for a new wardrobe.' She hailed another taxi.

She was closing up one trunk. She went to the closet to see if there was anything left she might want to take. She jumped when she saw the suit hanging in the back. Realizing it was only Thomas' suit, she shut the door. When she met him, he was sitting by himself at a restaurant. He was very handsome and a little unnerving considering his expression.

He looked up at her before she could avert her eyes. He smiled and strode over and introduced himself. She liked his smooth deep voice and his captivating eyes. After an hour talking, they went back to her apartment. Afterwards, whenever he came to town, he would pay her a visit.

She liked, that he listened to her talk about her job and Caleb. He never appeared jealous, that she loved another. When Emily came to town, he told her he would get Caleb away from Emily if she would help him. For, awhile, it was easy tearing up her letters and not sending, Caleb's. It was easy enough to ward off, her phone calls. When she appeared at the office, Billie, had to be firm, that Caleb wasn't available

It was a close call, considering Caleb was in his office with clients. For a second, she almost felt sorry for Emily. But, Caleb didn't need to get mixed up with the likes of her. Emily, eventually gave up. Caleb wouldn't let her go. He thought going to war would help him forget. He was away for so long. Then he returned with a limp. Billie blamed Emily for driving him to peril.

Imagining what Emily suffered at Thomas' hands made her cringe. Now, Thomas would be punished and by two- thirty she would be on her way to Los Angeles. It was one o'clock now. Plenty of time to bathe and dress. As she ran the tub, she heard a knock on the door.

CHAPTER 16

T HOMAS WILL WATCHED AS Caleb pulled away. He had to bide his time after he was arrested. His hearing was quick and was immediately sent to the asylum. He was fearful they would send him to the hell hole, but to his surprise they kept him in solitary until they could figure out what to do with him. He was let out for meals and to exercise. They were sure that he would behave and brought him to the main ward after three days. He was as docile as a little lamb. Even his psychiatrist was pleased that he was truly repentant and wanted to get better. He'd been given his chores to carry out. He was grateful the place hadn't changed since he was there last.

Work and discipline, work right up to bedtime. Ten minutes with a doctor once a week were the criteria to keep the sheep in line. Not make them better. Kept in line. It was on such an occasion that he was mopping out the break room. He saw the evening newspaper someone had left. It had the story of Caleb and Colleen. They were going to California, how interesting.

At night, they kept a small staff at the facility. Taking comfort that everyone would be asleep, there was no need for the army employed during the day. By eleven o'clock, all the patients were either chained, drugged or tied to their beds. A guard was escorting Thomas to his bed when he lashed out. He elbowed the orderly in the nose, blood flew everywhere. "You bastard."

He, rather quickly, brought out his baton and hit Thomas in the stomach. Thomas doubled over with great pain. The guard called in two orderlies who rushed to his aid. When they saw who it was, it didn't surprise them. "I wondered how long it would take him." Number one orderly said. He told the guard to go to the infirmary and have them look at his nose.

They dragged Thomas up to his feet and carried him to the stairwell. "It was only a matter of time." One orderly said to the other. "Yeah. I know the perfect place for this one. He should've been put down there in the first place." Thomas head was hanging down, they didn't see him smile. "We don't like having our break time interrupted, wise ass. This will teach you." They rounded the corner and faced the door to the hell hole.

Thomas drooped against the first orderly while the other unlocked the door. When the huge lock clanked over was when Thomas drove his shiv into the orderly's heart. He dropped to the floor. Thomas brought his fists up and hit the other in the back forcing his head on the door. Falling to his knees, Thomas grabbed the keys and slammed the orderly's head against the door once more, for good measure.

He had to move fast. He could hear the occupants inside beginning to stir. Shoving the stunned orderly in was no problem. The other, who was dying, and was dead weight, took some effort, but Thomas managed to sit him up. He stripped him of his shirt and tossed it into the basin. Pulling his shoes and pants off, he then stood him up and pushed him in. Locking the door, he looked thru the small window.

The first orderly was beginning to come around. Realizing where he was he struggled to his feet. Thomas was busy washing out what blood he could from the shirt. Satisfied, he wrung out the shirt and hung it on a chair. Changing into the orderly's pants and shoes, he heard the orderly whisper. "Please, let me out. Don't leave me here."

Thomas tied his shoelace and looked up at the pleading face. Thomas smiled. He unlocked the window he'd escaped from so long ago. Picking up the damp shirt, he pulled in on and picked up the keys. He walked over to the orderly's hopeful face and raised the keys to the window. In an instance the orderly vanished. They had gotten him. Thomas peeked in to see him being dragged away. He tossed the keys in.

Thomas made his way to Billie's apartment. It would be some time before the orderlies were missed and if one of the inmates figured out the keys, the rest of the staff would be kept busy reining them in. Standing across from her apartment house, Thomas looked about. Not a soul around. He hurried to the alley and made his way up the fire escape. Reaching the second floor, he raised the window and climbed in.

He rapped on the door softly. Listening he heard her making her way. "Who is it?" She asked. "Caleb." He whispered back. Immediately, the latches were thrown back. Her smile turned to horror when Thomas clamped his hand over her mouth and pushed her inside. Shutting the door, he whispered he would move his hand if she wouldn't scream. There were tears in her eyes as she nodded. "Surprise." He said cheerfully. Smiling at her worried face. "Aren't you going to say anything?"

She blundered, "I, I, I don't know what to say. It is a surprise." She managed a nervous smile for him. He chuckled, "Still hoping, ole Caleb is going to show up and forgive and forget. Take you away from all of this." She raised her chin defiantly. "No. That's all over now." Thomas saw the newspaper on the side table. "He's found his daughter. How sweet. He'll need a mother for her, now." He laughed. Billie glared at him.

"What do you want, Thomas?" He ignored her. "He found out about your efforts to keep him and the love of his life apart. That's too bad. What will you do now?"

"I'm going away."

"I see. So, you must've withdrawn the money."

"What else could I do? They fired me."

"I'm so sorry to hear that." He embraced her and kissed her forehead. "It hasn't been easy for you, I know." He felt her relax. "Things haven't worked out like they should, have they my darling?"

"No. He hates me now."

"Where will you go?" He stroked her back. She sighed. "I don't care." She looked at him. "Why not come with me. We'll have plenty to start over."

"Do you really want me?" He asked in a hurt voice. Billie lowered her eyes. "I know I said some hateful things at the police station. I was so upset."

"Now you've had a change of heart." He caressed her back. "I've had time to think. We were good together."

"Of course, we were. No reason why, we can't continue."

Billie put her arms around his neck. "I've missed you, Thomas." He kissed her deeply then carried her into the bedroom.

While Billie bathed, Thomas found the money. He brought out his suit from her closet. He was a little surprised she hadn't thrown it out. He smiled. He was glad he had one last time with her, she was very good. He lied on the bed waiting for her. She opened the bathroom door and was tying the sash to her robe. She smiled at his exquisite nude body stretched out. "All yours." She chirped brushing her hair.

He stood behind her with his arm around her waist while she applied her lipstick. "You should hurry, we should leave soon. "I still need to shave." He said and produced the straight razor he carried in his suit. Billie's eyes widened. "I've changed my mind about going with you." He held her tightly, bringing the razor to her throat. She let out a faint cry, a tear slid down her cheek. She looked at her reflection. The blade, tight against her skin. Her eyes danced from the razor to Thomas' icy gaze. As the clock struck two-thirty, he slid the blade across her throat. She gasped and her body collapsed in his embrace. He laid her in the tub to bleed out. Rinsing the razor, Thomas set about shaving his beard of thirty years.

CHAPTER 17

HE TURNED SIDE TO side admiring his features. The scar he'd obtained from Emily so long ago was evident. *'Poor Emily.'* He thought. A knock at the door startled him. He stepped softly to the door. Listening intently, he waited, then a key was being pushed under the door, footsteps faded in the hall. Thomas went to the window and pulled the shade back as to see the street below. For a moment he thought Caleb would come back. He was glad he didn't. Thomas didn't want to deal with him at the moment.

He looked back at Billie. He wanted to take a bath. The stench of the asylum annoyed him. He opened one of the trunks and dumped out the contents. Bringing her limp body over, he carefully laid her on her side. He rinsed out the tub and settled in for a nice soak. When he'd met Billie, she was sitting at a table looking morose. He made his move and she was happy with his attention. She was a handsome girl, also jealous and possessive. He could tell by the looks she'd given the poor waitress, who was merely doing her job. He liked her at once.

He would always visit when he came to town. She spoke endlessly about Caleb. He thought it strange she felt so comfortable doing so, since she was so accommodating in bed, with him. He, let her carry on about him. It didn't really matter to him. After knowing her for some time he trusted her enough to give her a key to the safe deposit box, in case anything happened to him. There wasn't much, he told her, just enough to cover any expenses. He never told her about his money or his private life.

He explained his frequent trips, telling her he was caring for an aging relative. She thought it sweet of him. She had passed his test by the numerous times he went to the bank to see if the money had been tampered with. It wasn't until, Emily had her fling with Caleb that she found out, he had a wife. She swore, she would do, whatever she could to keep them apart. She failed him in the end. They always failed him.

It was a shame, about Mr. Peaster. He really enjoyed his company. He had an inkling that he was snooping about the house. No matter what, he couldn't cause him to incriminate himself. He knew he wanted to leave. He had to do something to keep him. So, he let him see the remnants, of his own misdeeds. It amazed him how violent he became with those girls at Lettie's.

Strangling them was his favorite. The last time he wanted to try something new. Using his razor, to cut off the girls clothes. Only, he wasn't careful, at all.

The girl began to cry. He scared her with his rants. He endured her sobs until they became so loud he grew disgusted. He slashed her across the throat. Blood splattered his trousers. He pushed the girl away and sat on the bed. Looking at Thomas sitting across the room, he begged him. "Please, Mr. Will. Get Darby. Get her out of my sight." Thomas stood, putting on his robe and fetched Darby. When they returned, Mr. Peaster was passed out on the bed. Thomas Will thought it remarkable, he could block out so many killings. It had cost him plenty to replace them, but he did look forward to Mr. Peaster's enthusiasm.

It was too bad for Emily to have put so much trust in Mr.

Peaster. Thomas, had only ever wanted the best for Emily. He had promised her that he would give her the finest education. He, intended on showing her the world in their travels. When she met a man worthy of her, he had planned on handing over his fortune to her as a wedding gift. As it turned out, he wanted to wait until the twins were graduated before doing so. Either way, he was going to leave her financially sound as he moved back to the Phillippines.

If Emily hadn't been so impatient in helping Mr. Peaster, she would've been a very rich and alive woman. By the time Mr. Calloway tracked Thomas down in Pierce, Mr. Peaster was already talking to that horrible, Judge Rains. He was loading the car when the police arrived. A matter of ten minutes of going to get the boys changed things entirely. He, should have left them at Chauncey's. As much as he hated those two freaks, they did come in handy disposing of, Mr. Peaster. Had he known what the twins had done to Francis, he would have killed them himself, Toby managed just fine.

Thomas slipped on his coat and smoothed his tie. He smiled thinking of Chauncey's predicament. Why that man hounded him all his life, he never knew. He'd thought he'd gotten rid of him that night he saw him stumbling out of the bar. Only, he contacted him a few weeks later threatening to expose him killing Mr. Collin's. Thomas played along with his demands. He told him he'd paid for his house, even showing him a phoney deed.

He did pay his utilities and kept him in groceries. Only, Chauncey was more concerned with what he called his old age fund. Every month Thomas was to deposit funds to keep Chauncey quiet. He never questioned him because a monthly bank statement, Thomas forged, would arrive. Thomas chuckled over the surprise he would soon get once evicted. There was only one place the destitute went and that was the asylum. Old Chauncey. No son's, no money, no legs.

Thomas Will dumped the contents of a small bag Billie had, sitting on the dresser. Packing away his money, he snapped it shut and looked around one last time. Carefully, he stepped over the key, on the floor and closed the door. It was quiet in the building, that time of morning.

Things would be different with Colleen. He would only have to take her from Caleb and they would be on their way to the Philippines, to begin anew. He'd spent a lot of time there building his money and holdings there. He could give Colleen everything he'd planned for Emily. What a comfort she would be to him in his old age. Nobody would know them and they wouldn't be bothered.

Thomas Will walked softly down the lamp lit street towards the train station. Thomas, had always planned on getting Colleen out of that orphanage. It would be more fun ,tho, getting her from Caleb. Thomas would enjoy the fight. He often imagined Caleb's bruised and bleeding body slumped in a chair, beaten beyond recognition. He would ask him one last time to explain, before he slit his throat, "Why, when hired to do a job, such as following Emily, do you take my money, then do that job, so poorly?"